"The sunsets out here are gorgeous."

The sky was an array of colors. Oranges and reds filled the horizon, while the clouds above had turned purple and pink. Shades of blue lingered up high.

Harper's phone was out again as she took more pictures. "This is amazing."

Wyatt tried to focus on the sky, but the way the setting sun cast this glow across her face, he couldn't look away.

"You should get going. There aren't nearly as many streetlights in Eagle Springs as there are in Las Vegas. Everything always looks different in the dark."

She was quiet, studying him before she said, "Thanks for looking out for me. I'll call you tomorrow."

"Good night, Harper."

"Sleep well, Cowboy Wyatt," she said, backing away.

She had his mind whirling, which meant that this was not going to be easy. And he was going to have to find a way to explain why she was there to his family.

Wyatt's life had suddenly become more complicated than ever before...

Dear Reader,

I have to admit it—I love the Blackwells. When I was asked to help bring new Blackwells to life, I had to say yes. As much as I love Falcon Creek, Montana, I was excited to venture across the border and into Wyoming, where this new crop of the family resides.

Eagle Springs is a small town with a lot of heart. Wyatt Blackwell, however, thinks of his hometown as a bit suffocating. There's nothing new to learn and no opportunity to grow. That's what led him to hit the road and become a cowboy for hire. That is until his older sister calls him home to help save the family ranch. He agrees to return to Eagle Springs to do his part because family matters when you're a Blackwell.

Unlike Wyatt, Harper Hayes grew up constantly on the move. She learned quickly how to redefine herself so she could fit in. She also figured out how to find the best of everything in a new town.

Wyatt and Harper are that hero and heroine who give each other something they didn't think they could have. Of course, first they have to figure out how to hide an accidental marriage, save Eagle Springs and overcome a family feud!

Amy

HEARTWARMING

A Wyoming Secret Proposal

—

Amy Vastine

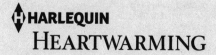
HARLEQUIN
HEARTWARMING

ISBN-13: 978-1-335-58462-5

Recycling programs
for this product may
not exist in your area.

A Wyoming Secret Proposal

Harlequin Enterprises ULC
22 Adelaide St. West, 41st Floor
Toronto, Ontario M5H 4E3, Canada
www.Harlequin.com

Printed in U.S.A.

Amy Vastine has been plotting stories in her head for as long as she can remember. An eternal optimist, she studied social work, hoping to teach others how to find their silver lining. Now she enjoys creating happily-ever-afters for all to read. Amy lives outside Chicago with her high-school-sweetheart husband, three teenagers who keep her on her toes and their two sweet but mischievous pups. Visit her at amyvastine.com.

Books by Amy Vastine

Harlequin Heartwarming

Stop the Wedding!

A Bridesmaid to Remember
His Brother's Bride
A Marriage of Inconvenience
The Sheriff's Valentine

Return of the Blackwell Brothers

The Rancher's Fake Fiancée

The Blackwell Sisters

Montana Wishes

Visit the Author Profile page at Harlequin.com for more titles.

This one is for my dad.
I know you're always with me.

CHAPTER ONE

September

"I WILL BET YOU fifty dollars that you run out of money before you finish your drink." Sam slapped Wyatt Blackwell on the back.

"Well, not the wisest bet you could make given if you win, I will have apparently lost all of my money and won't be able to pay up."

"Not all your money. Only that measly $200 you plan to bet with," Grant said with an eye roll.

The three cowboys-for-hire navigated their way through the crowded Las Vegas casino. Pop music played in the background while the sound of the electronic slot machines and the collective voices of the other gamblers swirled around them. The lack of windows made it impossible to know what time of day it was without checking a watch or phone. Sam swore they also pumped extra oxygen into the casinos so people would stay awake and feel more refreshed.

These three were used to wide open spaces and lots of fresh air. They had recently finished up a job on a ranch west of Las Vegas that had paid them well enough to have some extra to gamble away.

"Don't you worry about me, boys. Give me a couple hours and I'll turn this $200 into $400. I might even treat you two to a buffet," Wyatt said with a wink.

Wyatt loved a good game of blackjack, and he could easily kill a couple hours with what he had as long as he didn't sit at any of the high roller tables.

"I am going to actually have some fun with the extra money in my pocket and go play with the big boys tonight," Sam said, readjusting his hat. "I work hard. I play hard. That's the only way to live."

They all had worked hard. A cowboy's work was truly never done. That was why Wyatt had no trouble picking up work wherever he wandered. It didn't always pay exceptionally well, but that usually didn't matter so much. The only one Wyatt had to worry about was Wyatt. Unfortunately, his sister Corliss had changed that. He was now on the hook for twenty grand to bail his grandmother out of some big trouble, leaving him in Vegas on a budget.

This was his last hurrah before he drove himself and his camper, which he affectionately referred to as Betty, back to Eagle Springs, Wyoming, to work his butt off for zero dollars. Free labor was the only way Corliss was getting twenty thousand out of him.

"You have fun over there. I'll have my own fun over here." Wyatt nodded in the direction of the five-dollar blackjack tables.

"I'm going to test my luck at the slots," Grant said after finishing off his first drink of the night. "I'll meet you guys back at the Leopard Lounge when you're done. I hope you win, Blackwell. I want that free dinner."

Wyatt watched as the two of them sauntered away, craning their necks to get a look at a threesome of ladies who had walked in looking like a million bucks. The redheaded one had her phone in hand and was clearly filming the long-legged blonde. The blonde had on a sparkly sequined mini dress and heels that made her several inches taller than she was. Wyatt shook his head; a woman could break an ankle in those things if she wasn't careful.

The woman in the sparkly dress spoke like she was some sort of reporter, sharing facts about the hotel and casino they were in. Wyatt had never seen a reporter dressed like that before. The third woman was slender, her hair was bleached and cut short. She held up some kind of circular sunshade, tilting it toward the one that sparkled.

"How was that?" Sparkle asked her friends as he passed by them to get to the blackjack table.

"Good. You sounded really knowledgeable. The lighting in here isn't great, though. Even with Janelle holding the light reflector on you, you look sort of yellow."

When Wyatt looked at her, he didn't see yellow. He saw a lightly sun-kissed apricot. She took good care of herself and didn't let her body bake in the hot sun like he did. Maybe she was a reporter. There were all kinds in Vegas.

Wyatt found an empty spot at the five-dollar table and set his two hundred dollars down on the table, waiting for his chips and some cards. As the dealer got him set up, the waitress came by and asked him if he needed a drink. He decided to prove Sam wrong and downed the rest of his whiskey sour and asked her for another.

Two hands, two losses. Things weren't starting off as well as he had hoped. The guy who had won the last two hands decided to call it quits while he was ahead, leaving Wyatt alone at the table with the dealer. His drink arrived at the same time the blonde reporter lady and her friends appeared. She slid into the seat next to him.

"Hi," she said, her cheeks the prettiest color of pink.

"Howdy," he said with a tip of his hat.

"Are you a real cowboy or do you just play one on TV?" she asked as she set a hundred dollars down on the table.

A grin stretched across Wyatt's face. He rubbed one of his chips between his fingers and his thumb. She was entertaining. "I ain't never been on TV, so I guess that makes me one of those real ones."

"Would you like to be on TV? Well, not really TV, but I can put you on the internet at least. I'm Harper Hayes, maybe you've heard of me?"

Wyatt had never heard of anyone by the name Harper Hayes before. He wasn't sure why he would have since he spent almost zero time on the internet. He didn't own a computer and his phone was not one of the smart ones.

Wyatt checked his cards and asked for a hit. The new card gave him a solid nineteen. He stayed. "Sorry, Miss Hayes. Your name doesn't ring any bells. I'm Wyatt Blackwell, maybe you've heard of me?"

She shook her head and laughed. "Are you famous for something?" She checked her cards and chose to stay.

"Not that I'm aware of," he replied.

"Then why would I have heard of you?"

"No clue." Wyatt ducked his head and chuckled. "Maybe we should start over. Wyatt Blackwell." He offered his hand and she shook it.

"Harper Hayes."

"It's nice to make your acquaintance, Miss Hayes."

"These are my friends," Harper said, acknowledging the two women standing behind her. "Sloane is my camera operator and Janelle here makes sure the lighting is the best it can be, given what we have to work with here." The two ladies smiled and waved. "We're making a video about this casino and hotel. We thought it might be fun to have a real cowboy teach us a little about blackjack. You game?"

The dealer flipped over his cards, adding a jack to a nine. Wyatt groaned and tossed his cards down. Harper flipped hers. She had two kings, beating the House.

"I'm not sure you need much teaching," he remarked.

She feigned innocence, fluttering those long dark eyelashes at him. "Beginner's luck."

"Yeah, right," he said with a nod.

"Come on. It'll be fun."

Wyatt wasn't much for being the center of attention, but he did enjoy trying new things and he sure didn't mind the company of a pretty woman.

"Let's do it," he replied to the three women's glee.

"You can't video record at the tables or

anywhere in the gaming area, ma'am," the dealer said.

"Selfies?" she asked and seemed excited when he said yes.

"Selfies?" Wyatt questioned.

Harper threw her arm over his shoulders and put her cheek right up against his. She smelled good, like the wildflowers his mother used to gather up and put in the vase on the kitchen table all summer long. She held out her phone in front of them and their picture was there on the screen.

"Smile, Cowboy Wyatt."

He tried, but man, did he want to bury his nose in her neck and inhale until his lungs were full of that scent.

"Wow, you sure you've never done print or film work before? You smize better than the pros." Showing her friends, Sloane fanned herself and Janelle nodded approvingly.

"Should I know what smize means?"

She held up her phone so he could see their photo. "That right there is smizing. It's that hint of a smile. It's your eyes. You have gorgeous eyes. Those eyes have broken hearts, haven't they?"

Wyatt never stuck around anywhere

long enough for anyone to get too attached. "Never."

Harper narrowed her eyes suspiciously. "Liar."

He showed her the ropes even though blackjack wasn't that complicated. If she could count to twenty-one, she could figure it out. He did have to show her when to split and when to double down. She was a quick learner when it came to paying attention to the dealer's face-up cards. Once she felt confident enough, he stopped helping and got back in the game. After an hour, she was up and he was almost out of money.

The luckier Harper got, the more people joined their table. The more she won, the more the waitress came by, offering to get them more drinks. The more they drank, the bolder she got. They managed to turn her $100 into $500.

"What do you think? Bet it all?" she asked Wyatt.

"Do it!" her friends goaded her.

"Can you afford to lose it all?" he asked her.

"With you by my side, I can't possibly lose," she said, pushing all her chips into the betting circle.

No pressure.

Harper was dealt two nines, but the dealer had a seven showing. Wyatt wanted to tell her to stand, but she split it—a risky move. She most likely would have won if she had left it. The dealer passed her two more cards. She got a queen for nineteen on one and a two on the other. She stole a glance Wyatt's way. Eleven was good. Eleven was very good.

She hit.

The dealer flipped over her next card. King! She leaped up out of her chair as soon as it hit the table. Harper flung herself at Wyatt and planted a big ol' kiss right on his mouth. He was so shocked he didn't get to appreciate the way she felt in his arms or the way her lips fit perfectly against his before it was over. She was jumping up and down with her friends and high-fiving the people gathered around the table to watch her.

Someone nudged Wyatt's shoulder. Sam and Grant were behind him, smirking. "You sure picked the right seat at the table," Sam said.

"Can you believe it?" Harper's eyes were lit.

"You are one lucky lady," Wyatt acknowledged.

"Oh come on, you were a good teacher."

"Did Wyatt make a friend at the blackjack table?" Grant asked.

Wyatt introduced his friends to Harper and her friends, hoping Sam and Grant would behave themselves. Working on a ranch, the only females these three had been around were cattle.

"You guys have to let me buy you dinner," Harper offered.

"Absolutely!" Grant was more than happy to accept the invitation.

"Great idea," Sam chimed in. They both stared hard at Wyatt, pleading with their eyes to let them go to dinner.

Wyatt had more drinks than he had planned for and the warm feeling made it impossible to say no to this proposition. He didn't even really care if Sam and Grant embarrassed him. Spending time with Harper was his sole focus. He got that one kiss and, man, was he hoping for another.

Harper cashed in her chips and with the new money in her pocket, the six of them went to dinner. More selfies were taken, more stories were told and the laughs were abundant.

"So how long are you staying here in Vegas?" Harper asked Wyatt.

"I leave tomorrow."

Her bottom lip jutted out and she tipped her head to her chest. She had the cutest little upturned nose. "Tomorrow?"

"Gotta head home to Wyoming. My family needs me."

"Wyoming? Where in Wyoming?"

"It's a small town. I doubt you've ever heard of it."

"My mom and stepdad are in Eagle Springs. Have you heard of that?"

Wyatt didn't know if it was the noise or the bright lights or the fact that he couldn't stop staring at her lips because there was no way she said her family was from Eagle Springs. "Are you messing with me?"

Her green eyes were getting squintier by the minute. "No, why?"

"You're from Eagle Springs, Wyoming?"

"I'm not from there, no, no, no, I'm from Los Angeles, but my mom lives there now." She snorted when she laughed. "Serena, that's my mom by the way, didn't realize she was going to be living in the middle of nowhere when she caught this last guy. She had to buy cowboy boots. Cowboy boots… on my mother's feet. It's a thing to see." She snorted again.

The middle of nowhere was definitely one way to describe Eagle Springs, but people from big cities in California might think anywhere in Wyoming was the middle of nowhere. "So you've visited her there? You've been to Eagle Springs?" Wyatt asked, trying to get her back on track.

"Oh, I've been there," she said waggling her pointer finger at him. "When she got married, I was there for a *whole* week. Downtown they have this statue of a bull and there's this ice cream shop that has the best ice cream on the planet."

Holy cow. She really had been there. "You've been to Tucker's Ice Cream Shop?"

"That was it. Tucker. You know, Tucker told me I was his favorite customer."

Wyatt shook his head. "No way. No way! I know Tucker. I grew up in Eagle Springs and *I* am Tucker's favorite customer. All I have to do is walk in and he starts scooping my favorite flavor into a cake cone. Not a sugar cone because he knows I don't like those."

"Get out of here!" Harper smacked him on the shoulder before taking him by the hand. "It's true we live in a smaller world than we think. Meeting you was destiny, Cowboy Wyatt."

Wyatt wasn't sure he believed in destiny, but he liked the way her hand felt in his. "Small world is right."

"I wish you weren't leaving tomorrow," she added. "I could get used to your smize."

Wyatt felt one side of his mouth form a crooked grin. He leaned in close. "At least we have tonight."

"That we do." She tapped him on the nose.

WHEN WYATT WOKE UP the next morning, dinner was the last thing that he could remember. His head hurt and his body was sore. The gray-and-blue carpet he was sprawled out on was not familiar. Had he fallen out of bed? He rubbed the sleep out of his eyes and realized he was not in his room. Where was he?

He tried to make sense of what happened after dinner, but everything was sort of a blur of colors and light. He remembered feelings more than events. Laughter. There had been a lot of laughter. Joy. Joy was not a feeling he had very often. Kissing. Oh man, there had been more kissing. He really wished he could remember that part a bit better.

Wait. This was Harper's room. They had come back here and there had been kissing. Nothing more than kissing, though. He remembered telling her, "Married or not, I won't sleep with you on the first date."

That was a weird thing to say, but at least he had been a gentleman. He sat up and rubbed his sore neck. She had given him two pillows and a bedsheet, but it had still been a rough night's sleep.

He had a long drive ahead of him and no time to waste on this hangover. He pulled himself up off the floor and straightened his clothes.

Peacefully curled up on her side with an eye mask covering those pretty green eyes was his sleeping beauty. She looked too cute to wake. Too bad their timing was so bad. He couldn't put off heading home. Maybe they'd see each other again. Had he been dreaming or had she mentioned Tucker's? There was little chance their paths would cross again. Wyatt was always on the move and, from what he could remember, so was she.

He found a pen and the hotel notepad by the phone and jotted her a few words, so she didn't think he ran out without saying goodbye.

Wyatt took one more good look at the woman who had managed to steal a little piece of his heart in one night. She was something else. Something he couldn't have, though. Wyoming was calling him home and there was no more time for being young and carefree. Wyatt had work to do, responsibilities to meet and bills to pay so his gran could stay put until the good Lord decided it was time for her to leave this world. Denny Blackwell wasn't ready to be done just yet, and since Wyatt was a betting man, he'd always put his money on his gran. Always.

CHAPTER TWO

HARPER'S HEAD THROBBED. That was the only thing she could comprehend as she lay in bed. The pain was that bad. She lifted her eye mask and promptly put it back in place. The light made the pain ten times worse. Why had she gotten so carried away last night? At least she had made it back to her room. Well, she hoped this was her room.

What if this isn't my room?

She clenched her eyes shut as she lifted the mask again. A quick peek told her she was safely in her room. Willing herself to rise up on one elbow, she felt around the bed until she found her phone. It wasn't plugged in, which meant it was surely out of power.

What a night it had been. She clearly remembered winning big at blackjack. She sort of remembered having dinner with a bunch of cowboys. She vaguely remembered kissing one of those cowboys. Wyatt. That was his name. He was handsome with dark brown hair that hid under a cowboy hat. He was kind of quiet in a charming way. What he didn't say with words, he said with those eyes of his. She could picture those eyes staring into hers. Hazel eyes that were a bit more green than brown.

Her whole body felt warm. Maybe it was thinking about Wyatt; maybe it was the aftereffects of her night out. She kicked off the heavy white feather down duvet and silently begged the pain in her head to stop.

She was in desperate need of some water. Her mouth was dry, causing her tongue to feel like sandpaper. She slid the eye mask up on her forehead and waited for her eyes to adjust to the sunlight streaming in from the window. She must have forgotten to put the shade down.

Never again. She would never let herself drink that much ever again. Sitting up was still a struggle, but she managed. Two pillows sat on the floor beside the bed along with a sheet. Had she knocked those off in the middle of the night? She wasn't usually a restless sleeper.

The faint memory of kissing Wyatt in this

very room forced its way into her consciousness. Not only had she kissed him, she had practically thrown herself at him. He didn't give in to her advances. He had refused to take advantage of her, even though she had desperately wanted him to. He had slept on the floor. She remembered that much.

Her heart squeezed in her chest as she came to the realization Wyatt wasn't there anymore. He had told her he was leaving to go home today. The one time she met a legitimately upstanding and decent guy, he had to be headed out of town never to be seen or heard from again. Maybe it was for the best. She would have ended up breaking his heart in the end because Harper didn't believe in tying herself down to a man. In fact, she planned to be single for the rest of her life.

She found her phone-charger cord and plugged it into her dead phone. It would be ready to use once she was out of the shower and feeling more like a human. There on the nightstand sat a bottle of water. *Hallelujah*. Harper couldn't open it or drink it fast enough. Refreshed, she wiped her mouth and noticed the note with her name scrawled across it sitting beside where the water had been. She unfolded the piece of paper.

Thanks for making my night in Vegas one I won't soon forget. If you ever make it back to Eagle Springs, maybe we can settle this who's Tucker's favorite customer debate once and for all.—Wyatt

Eagle Springs? Harper rubbed the heel of her hand against her throbbing temple. Did he tell her he was from Eagle Springs? She didn't believe in coincidences. Not that she had any intentions of ever going back to that town. Thanks to her night with Cowboy Wyatt, she was inspired to make her next trip somewhere more romantic. In all likelihood, her mother would probably be divorced before Harper could make it back to Wyoming anyways. Serena was not cut out for living in the Wild West.

Harper needed to pull herself together. Quick. She attempted to stand and made it all the way to the window to close the drapes and return the room to a peaceful darkness. One thing about Vegas, it loved to mess with your sense of time. You could sleep all day and stay up all night.

Cowboy Wyatt lingered in her mind. Hanging out with him and his friends was a one night only adventure—another very Vegas thing. Last night would only live on through her social media post about him when she finished editing the footage from her big blackjack win. She was going to make him famous and he'd probably never know it. The man didn't even own a smartphone. How did he survive?

She needed a shower if she was going to get over this hangover. Before she could make it to the bathroom, there was a terrible pounding on her door.

"Please stop!" she shouted much to her head's dismay. Whoever it was didn't listen to her plea, so she pulled herself up and shuffled to the door. "Okay, okay. I'm coming. Stop knocking."

Harper pulled the door open and Sloane and Janelle pushed their way in without even saying good morning.

"Are you alone?" Sloane asked, her eyes scanning the room as if someone might suddenly appear.

"Is he here?" Janelle asked, peeking into the bathroom and frowning when she found it was empty. "Where is he?"

"Where is who? Wyatt?"

"Um, yeah, Wyatt." Janelle threw her hands up like that was a ridiculous question.

Of course they knew that he had spent the night. "He's gone."

"What are you two going to do?" Sloane asked, sitting on the bed and staring at Harper expectantly.

Janelle picked up one of the pillows on the floor. "Did you guys talk about it this morning? How does he feel about it?"

Harper had no idea why they thought she needed to talk to Wyatt. Nothing had happened besides some kissing and him sleeping on the floor. "Wyatt and I haven't talked since last night."

Sloane and Janelle exchanged a look. "I can't imagine what you're going to do. I've been thinking about it all morning and I have no advice for you. What do you think you should do? You have to have a plan."

Harper was having a hard enough time standing still given that the room was slightly spinning. She couldn't answer their nonsensical questions on top of that. "Do about what? What are you two talking about?"

"Oh my gosh," Sloane said, her eyes wide. "Janelle, she doesn't remember."

Janelle's expression shifted from concern to surprise. "Harper, please tell me you remember. Oh goodness, do you not remember?"

"Remember what?"

"Remember what happened last night," Sloane replied.

Harper needed to sit down. She carefully lowered herself down next to Sloane. "I remember winning at cards. I remember making out with Wyatt, who I remember is a really cute, sweet guy. I remember bringing him back to my room and him telling me he would not sleep in the same bed as me. Thankfully, I don't remember how embarrassing that probably was."

"You guys didn't...?" Sloane seemed shocked.

"No, we didn't."

"Wow." Janelle sat down on the bed on the other side of Sloane. "That's not what I expected after what happened."

"After *what* happened?" Harper repeated.

"I can't believe you have to find out this way." Sloane tapped on her phone and held it out. "See for yourself."

Harper took the phone. Sloane had pulled up Harper's Instagram account. Harper scrolled through the pictures in the last post that she had apparently tagged "#it'sofficial." There were several pretty adorable selfies with Wyatt. There was a full-length picture of him with his cowboy hat on and those eyes were smizing like there was no tomorrow. He was drop-dead gorgeous. There were pictures of her and him. Why was she holding flowers? She kept scrolling to the end where there was a video. Harper watched in complete horror as she witnessed her and Wyatt standing in front of a man dressed like Elvis.

"I now pronounce you husband and wife," the man said. "You may kiss the bride."

Wyatt tried to dip her, but they almost lost their footing. One of his friends righted them and Wyatt smiled at her before planting a kiss on her lips. Did he just kiss the bride? Was she the bride? Harper felt like she was going to pass out.

"Congratulations?" Janelle tried.

Harper dropped the phone and held her left hand up. There was no ring. These two had to be messing with her. "This is a joke, right?"

"You two didn't bother with rings. They wanted an outrageous amount of money for fourteen-karat gold bands. I wouldn't let you do that. Wyatt promised to get you a diamond in the morning," Janelle explained.

"Did you two let me get married last night?" She may have sounded a bit hysterical.

"Let you?" Sloane huffed. "You two were not going to be talked out of it. You kept going on and on about how it was fate and you were meant to be together."

That was impossible. Harper never wanted to get married. Marriage was a joke. Her mother had done it more times than any person should. If there was one thing Harper never wanted to do, it was be like her mother. She had promised herself she would never get married, therefore never get divorced.

"I'm gonna have to get a divorce." This was her worst nightmare come true.

"Is that what Wyatt wants?" Sloane asked.

Wyatt? Why should she care what he wanted? Wyatt left. Wyatt was on his way to Wyoming. Did he even remember what happened? His note sure didn't give any hints that he recalled making her his wife the night before.

"I don't even think he knows we're married. He left while I was still sleeping. Oh my gosh. What am I going to do?"

"That's what I've been asking!" Sloane said, throwing her hands up.

"We don't know what you should do," Janelle said. "All I know is that this post is blowing up. People are eating up this spontaneous romance. You were posting about him all night. Look at all the comments."

Harper picked Sloane's phone back up and scrolled through the half a dozen posts she'd put up overnight. She clicked on some of the comments. There were hundreds. Most of them were wishing her congratulations. Some were commenting on how cute she and Wyatt were together. Her followers were in love with her being in love. Only they had no idea that love had nothing to do with what happened last night.

She fell back on the bed and covered her eyes with her arm. "People are going to freak out if I tell them that this was a huge mistake."

"Your followers love this," Janelle said. "I don't know how you can spin it so they still love you after you break Cowboy Wyatt's heart. They really love him."

"Maybe you make him break your heart," Sloane suggested. "He can be the bad guy who asks for a divorce. You'll put out a statement asking for privacy during this difficult time and say something like, you respect his decision and always wish him the best. You know, make it look like you're the bigger person."

"Well, he's definitely going to be asking for a divorce. Why wouldn't he? Seeing as how we barely know one another!" Harper felt like her world was spinning out of control. She could feel an anxiety attack coming on. "I don't have his phone number. I don't even remember his last name. How am I even going to tell him that we need a divorce?"

"You know where he's headed, right? I guess you're going to have to start there,"

Sloane said, taking her phone. "You could do a whole series on living in Wyoming. It could be great."

"I am not living in Wyoming."

"Of course not," Sloane said. "But you need to make people think you are until the time is right to have Wyatt divorce you and then post about how you're coping with your heartbreak in Paris or something."

"Or Bali," Janelle suggested.

Sloane sighed happily. "Oh, Bali. That could be fun."

Harper had to think this through. That would have been easier if she wasn't nursing the worst hangover of all time. The facts were simple though; she was married to a guy who didn't even know they were married and had left town to go back to Wyoming. She had millions of followers thinking she was in love and got married because she was in love. Her reputation was at risk.

Harper prided herself in being real with her followers. She gave people her honest opinions and tried to be authentic in everything she did. Posting that she had married the man of her dreams was not honest, but she had to protect her online image. She could not look like a complete flake who married some random guy during a girls' night out adventure in Vegas.

This marriage had to appear somewhat legitimate if she was going to come out of this with any credibility on the other side. That meant she needed to get on the next plane to Wyoming and hunt down her husband, to ask him to go along with her wild plan to pretend to be married until it was okay not to be married.

How long would they need to pretend for? Two weeks? Three? What was her mother going to say? She couldn't tell her mother. This was the first time she was thankful that of her millions of social media followers, her mother was not one of them. The only time her mom cared about the internet was when she had to make a dating profile.

"How long do celebrities stay married when they make a huge mistake like this?" Harper asked.

Janelle did a quick internet search. "Some have gotten it annulled right away, but those would be the ones people are still talking about. Looks like most last anywhere from days to months. None of them make it a year. I'd say you'd be fine in a month."

Harper held her aching head in her hands. "A month? I can't pretend to be happily married for a month."

"You can pretend to do anything for a month," Janelle said. "Unless you want to post the truth. You can film the morning-after confessional. Tell everyone how you didn't even realize you were married until you watched the video this morning."

Just the thought of it was humiliating. Harper needed to clean up this mess but in a way that wouldn't cost her the reputation she had made for herself.

"I can do anything for a month."

"That's the spirit," Sloane said, giving her a pat on the back. "I can start looking for flights to Wyoming for you if you want me to."

"No, I'll figure it out. He was driving if I'm not mistaken." Harper wished things weren't so unclear. When she tried to search her memories, she felt like she was roaming around in fog, only able to see a few inches in front of her. "I think he said he was driving with someone named... Betty."

Janelle and Sloane both looked up from their phones. "Who's Betty?"

CHAPTER THREE

"COME ON, BETTY. How can you do this to me? I was counting on you. You can't fall apart on me now." Wyatt lifted his hat and wiped the sweat dripping down his forehead. He was fifteen miles outside of Eagle Springs when his aging camper trailer decided to get a flat tire. She had successfully gone over six hundred miles yesterday, but today, she decided to give out.

Good thing he hadn't kept driving last night. This would have been difficult to fix on this highway in the dark. Wyatt had needed to get some sleep, so he pulled over at a rest stop and did just that—rested for a few hours. Resting up was a good plan since he had a suspicion that he was going to be on the clock the second he stepped foot inside the fences of the Flying Spur Ranch.

Wyatt's phone rang in his pocket just as he got Betty raised up on the jack. He pulled it out, knowing better than not to answer his phone these days. His grandmother's illness had him worried and the only ones who ever called him were his family.

Corliss barely waited for him to say hello when he answered. "What's your ETA? I thought you'd be here by now. I can really use your help today."

Just as Wyatt had predicted, there would be no rest for a weary traveler. His oldest sister planned to put him right to work. "I'm not far. I should be there in less than a half hour."

"Half hour? Didn't you get up early and hit the road?"

It wasn't even nine in the morning. He was well aware that work on the ranch started at sunrise, but it wasn't like he was going to be pulling in at dinnertime. "As soon as I finish changing this flat tire on Betty, I'll be back on the road."

"You got a flat? I can't believe you trek that old camper all over the place. Don't these ranches you work on have bunkhouses?"

"I spent my entire life living with way too many people in one house. I'm a grown man who shouldn't have to fight for a few minutes in the bathroom like I did as a kid. I cherish my privacy. Betty is my saving grace. I will take her everywhere as long as she will let me."

"Does that mean you aren't planning on staying in the house while you're here? I made up a bed for you."

"Sorry, sis. Don't you need all those rooms now that you're married and have a new stepdaughter?" Corliss had shocked everyone by marrying her childhood best friend last month. Wyatt didn't completely understand it even though his other sister, Adele, tried to explain it to him. All he knew was that Corliss's family had doubled in size since the last time he had seen her. That meant he was staying with Betty.

"Well, you were going to be sharing a room with Mason."

Of course, there was no room for him. She'd planned to put him in a room with her thirteen-year-old son. Being the youngest of five meant he had always been the one who had to share; nothing was ever his own. He loved his nephew, but he sure wasn't going to share space with a teenager. "You can tell Mason that he doesn't have to share with his

uncle Wyatt. That should make me his favorite uncle."

Corliss laughed. "Given the argument we
had the other day about it, you may be right.
He didn't like it when I told him he either
had to share with you or Olivia."

That seemed like a no-brainer. His uncle
or his young stepsister? Uncle Wyatt had to
be the easy choice in that competition. "All
right. Let me get back to work so I can get
on the road and you can put me to work."

"Be safe. See you soon," his sister said
before hanging up.

Being home was going to be a little bit
different this time. Besides Corliss's new
family, Wyatt's oldest brother, Nash, was
home. Divorced and hopefully sober, Nash
had a lot of work to do training some
horses Corliss managed to buy thanks to
their grandmother's brother. Elias Blackwell was apparently another addition to
the ranch since Wyatt had been there last.
Gran's brother decided to stick around and
pitch in where he could. Not sure how much
help some guy in his eighties was going to
be, but Wyatt would surely need all the assistance he could get. Corliss had to let go

all the other ranch hands. Wyatt was going to be doing the work of half a dozen employees.

He finished putting the spare on Betty and climbed back in his truck. Eagle Springs was his next stop. Hopefully, this plan his sister came up with would be enough to save the ranch. He might not want to work there permanently, but it was still home. He couldn't imagine his gran living anywhere else. She was the heart of that place. Eagle Springs wouldn't be what it was if it wasn't for Denny Blackwell.

The ranch was on the north side of town, which meant that Wyatt had to go through the downtown area to get where he was going. He smiled as he passed Tucker's. What were the chances that he might ever run into Harper there? He probably would have had a better shot at winning a million dollars in Vegas than of bumping into her again. One thing was for sure; he planned on giving Tucker some flack for telling other customers they were his favorite. Wyatt did not like to share—bedrooms, bathrooms or titles.

The Flying Spur looked the same as he

pulled into the private drive. Gran had owned this place for as long as she could remember. She had always dreamed of it being in the family for generations. Wyatt hated the thought of it belonging to anyone else.

He parked in front of the main house. Saying hello to everyone would be his first order of business and then he'd set Betty up out by the bunkhouse where he could tap into the water and the electricity. Corliss stood on the front porch, hands on her hips, looking like the boss she had always been. Corliss had a knack for giving orders. She used to do it all the time when they were little. She kept them in line, even Nash, who was only a year younger than her.

"Made it. Don't tell me I don't have time to say hello to Gran before you put me to work."

Corliss's little Jack Russell terrier named Arrow came racing down the stairs to greet the newcomer. Wyatt bent down and gave Arrow the attention the little dog constantly craved. She could be annoying but was highly effective in catching mice in the barn.

"Of course I'm going to let you say hello," Corliss said. "But don't get any ideas about using the bathroom or stopping in the kitchen for a quick snack. There's work to be done and you're all I got."

Wyatt cocked his head and waited a second to make sure she was joking. Corliss's face broke into a big smile and she opened her arms. "I'm kidding. Get over here and give me a hug."

Wyatt climbed the porch steps two at a time and wrapped his sister up in an embrace. "You had me for a second. I believed you'd stop me from going into the kitchen, but I wasn't sure you'd deny a man a few minutes in the bathroom."

Corliss pulled back and flicked the brim of his hat. "Funny, little brother, I remember when you were a little kid and you used to hide in the barn, hoping Mom wouldn't notice so you could sleep out there."

Wyatt readjusted his hat and ducked his head. "Yeah, yeah. Well, I'm not a kid anymore."

"No, you aren't. Come inside. There's a couple extra biscuits leftover from breakfast with your name on 'em."

Biscuits loaded up with butter and jam sounded better than pretty much anything

Wyatt had eaten in a long time. Except for his celebratory dinner with Harper and her friends. From what he could remember, that was quite the meal.

"You didn't by chance win big in Vegas and forget to tell me?" Corliss asked as they entered the house.

"Trust me—I wouldn't have kept that a secret."

"Uncle Wyatt!" Mason, Corliss's son, came out of the kitchen holding what Wyatt hoped wasn't the last of the biscuits. He was followed by Ryder Talbot and a little girl that Wyatt assumed was his daughter. Corliss had a husband. That was going to take some getting used to.

"How's it going, bud?" Wyatt asked Mason.

"Good. I made the school soccer team this fall. I'm pretty excited."

"Nice work." Wyatt gave his nephew a high five. "And who is this?" He crouched down to get eye to eye with the newest member of the family.

"I'm Olivia."

"Nice to meet you, Olivia." He held out his hand and she shook it. "I guess I am your uncle Wyatt."

"Mason said you're cool."

"Your brother is a smart guy." Wyatt stood back up. "Smart and tall. Did you grow again while I was gone? It won't be long before you're taller than your mom."

"He might be taller than me someday, but I'll always be older and wiser." Corliss ruffled Mason's hair. "That means I'll always be the one in charge."

Wyatt laughed. "We all know better than to even think about usurping any of your power, Corliss."

"What's this about Corliss's power?" Nash asked, coming in from the front hall. "Is she a superhero or something that I'm not aware of?"

"She wishes," Mason said with a smirk.

"How many times have you accused your mom of having eyes in the back of her head?" Ryder asked. "If that's not a superpower, I don't know what is."

"He's got you there, Mason," Nash said before putting both his hands on Wyatt's shoulders and giving him a shake. "Welcome back, little brother. Glad you could find your way home to help us out around here."

"I didn't have much of a choice after Corliss let everyone else go. We know how you prefer to spend your time in the ring with the horses rather than get your hands dirty anywhere else on the ranch."

"Hey, your skills and my skills may be different, but the work is hard nonetheless."

"Don't forget that I'm here to help," Ryder said. Come November, Ryder would be the new fire chief in Eagle Springs. "I don't want you to feel like you're on your own around here."

Ryder and Corliss had been friends since they were little. As a kid, he had always been hanging around the Flying Spur. He wasn't a rancher, but he could ride and definitely assist Wyatt with the cattle.

"I look forward to working with you. We need as much help as we can get around here."

"We're going to be fine," Corliss said. "Things are going to work out just as we planned. They have to. Gran's depending on us."

Everyone got quiet for a second. The possibility of losing the ranch was too much for any of them to handle. Wyatt knew that his brother and sister were feeling the same pressure he did. They needed to come through for their grandmother. Denny Blackwell would die knowing her grandkids did everything they could to keep this ranch in the family.

Wyatt cleared his throat. "Speaking of Gran, where is she?" He tried to see past Ryder and into the kitchen.

"She's on her morning walk," Corliss replied. "She and Big E have started walking the property in the mornings and then they end up at his RV for some coffee."

Denny and her brother were spending the mornings together? "I thought she was trying to get him to leave."

"Oh, she tried," Nash said with a laugh. "That didn't go so well."

"You know how stubborn Gran is?" Corliss asked with a grimace. "Her brother is possibly more so. Maybe it's genetic."

"Ha!" Ryder let out a chuckle. "Maybe? I'm pretty sure that if you look up *stubborn* in the dictionary, you'll find Blackwell is a synonym." All three Blackwells glared at him, and he quickly tried to backpedal. "I mean, you know, I'm going to…um…finish cleaning up breakfast."

Once Ryder was back in the kitchen, the Blackwell siblings shared a laugh. Wyatt had been surprised by Corliss's elopement—not because of who she married but simply because she did it without any warning. Ryder was a good man, though. He'd be a fine stepdad to Mason. That was important.

"Were those the last of the biscuits?" Wyatt asked Mason, who was finishing off one of them.

"Um…" His guilty glance told Wyatt all he needed to know. "Do you wan' 'is one?" he mumbled with his mouth full.

Wyatt shook his head. Now that he was back home, he needed to remember that if he was the last one to the kitchen table, there might not be anything left to eat. "I need to go find Gran."

"I'll walk with you," Corliss offered.

"Nah," he waved her off. "You stay here and I promise to come find you for my to-do list as soon as I finish catching up with Gran."

"It's a long list. I hope you're ready for this."

"I can handle anything you want to throw at me."

Nash smacked him on the back. "You are so going to regret saying that."

Wyatt wasn't afraid of hard work. It felt good to be productive. He loved the fresh air and the sunshine on his skin. He loved the way working on a ranch made his body strong and kept his mind clear. What he didn't love was feeling tied down, and for the next couple months, he was tied to this place. It was the only way they were going to have enough money to pay off the mortgage.

He didn't have to go far to find his grandmother. She was standing beside Betty with her brother and Bow, Corliss's chocolate Lab.

"How old is this thing?" Elias asked.

"Not as old as you," Denny replied. She turned to look at Wyatt when the screen door slammed shut. "You made it."

She looked the same, which was good. He had worried she would look sickly, and he wasn't sure he could handle that. The Gran he knew was the toughest woman in the world. He couldn't remember her even catching a cold his entire life.

He jogged down the steps. "I made it. It's great to see you, Gran."

She let him wrap her up in a big hug. She felt a little smaller than the last time. She'd always been a sturdy lady. Today, she seemed a little bit wispier.

"I thought you would drive straight through and show up last night. What happened?" she asked when he let her go.

"I got tired. Stayed up too late the night before. You know how it is in Vegas. Can't tell if it's night or day inside those casinos."

"I hope you didn't do anything foolish," Gran said. She hated gambling. It was the one vice she'd always warned the kids to steer clear of. "That town has a way of making people forget themselves."

Wyatt couldn't remember the whole evening, but he didn't think he did anything that could come back to haunt him. "I was on my best behavior, Gran. Don't you worry."

"Oh goodness, life isn't worth living if you don't do something a little foolish now and again," Elias said.

"Don't you listen to a word he says, you hear me?" She turned to her brother. "You save your terrible advice for your grandchildren. Mine don't need your influence."

"Oh, you're going to try and tell me you didn't enjoy some of those times in your life when you cut loose and threw caution to the wind?"

"I was a very young, single mother who had to raise two boys and run a ranch all on her own. I didn't have time or the energy to throw caution anywhere."

"You forget I knew you before you were a wife and mother."

"I'm not doing this with you. Wyatt, this is my brother, Elias. Do not listen to a word he says. Do not get used to him being around. As soon as I can convince him that I have everything under control, he will be going back to his ranch in Montana. Hopefully, that will be sooner than later."

Elias rolled his eyes. "You are something else, Delaney."

"How many times do I have to tell you not to call me that?" she snapped, bristling at her given name. She was Denny to everyone and anyone. Wyatt had never heard her called anything else other than Mom and Gran.

Her brother puffed out his chest. "Don't call me Elias."

"I'll call you whatever I please. If you don't like it, you are free to go home." She pointed in the direction of the road.

He waved her off and turned his attention on Wyatt. "You can call me Big E, son. Pleasure to meet you," he said, tipping his hat.

"I've heard a lot about you lately. Nice to finally put a face to the name, sir."

"Don't call him sir. He doesn't deserve it," Gran said, shuffling to the porch. "Goodbye, *Elias*. Feel free to go home anytime."

"And miss out on all our quality time together? No way."

"Come on, Wyatt. Let's get in the house before he says anything else annoying."

Wyatt and Bow followed his grandmother back in the house. She still had that fire in her. This kidney problem hadn't changed that about her, and for that, he was grateful.

"You look good, Gran." At least better than he thought she would.

She patted his arm. "I appreciate you coming home to help out. If it wasn't for Brock Bedford and the bank, we wouldn't be in this position. Did you hear he had me arrested and thrown in jail?"

"Corliss may have mentioned that. It's a shame he's not thinking about all the things you've done for this town." Wyatt's grandmother had been the heart of Eagle Springs for decades. Besides being a successful rancher and business owner, she was mayor for a few years. Her focus had always been helping others so Eagle Springs could thrive. Most people were grateful for her dedication, but there were a few who disagreed with her vision for their small town. Maybe Brock was one of them.

"Corliss said that Big E said that there's maybe someone else who asked him to call in the loan?"

"Doesn't matter. I can't wait to walk into that bank and pay it off. Brock's going to totally lose it when we come up with the money."

Wyatt threw an arm over his grandma's shoulders and gave her a squeeze. "Well, I hope we're able to make that happen for you."

"Who's ready to get dirty?" Corliss met

them in the foyer and asked with a clap of her hands.

He was here to do what he could so Gran would get that satisfaction of ruining Brock's day. "You know me, sis. Dirty is the only way I like to be."

Corliss had no qualms about putting Wyatt right to work. There were fences to be fixed and a few cattle that needed to be moved. When things had gone south financially and they decided to let go the ranch hands, they had to sell some of the cows as well. There was no way that Wyatt alone could take care of a herd they were used to raising, but if Nash was going to train the best, they needed cattle for the cutting horses to practice with so they were skilled in handling a herd.

Wyatt put in a full day, and after dinner decided that he'd be the cool uncle and take the kids into town for some ice cream. His brother Levi was going to meet him there with his daughter as well. Mason and Olivia were thrilled with the idea.

"Did you guys know that I am Tucker's favorite customer?"

"How come?" Mason asked.

"He told me so. I've been going to Tucker's for ice cream since the place first opened. He knows what I want as soon as I walk in the door. He's never told you guys that you were his favorite, did he?"

"Not me," Olivia replied sadly. "I'm not his favorite."

Mason tried to make her feel better. "I'm not his favorite either, Liv. He's never said anything to me except to ask if I wanted whipped cream and a cherry."

All right, that meant that Tucker did not tell everyone they were his favorite. He definitely doubted that the man had told Harper she was his favorite. She'd probably only been there one time. How could she be his favorite when she wasn't a regular?

"Are you okay, Uncle Wyatt?" Mason asked.

"Yeah, why?"

"You just passed the turn to get downtown." Mason jerked a thumb over his shoulder.

Wyatt had been so distracted, he'd missed the turn. Why was he still bothering to think about a woman he was never going to see again? It was silly to be dwelling on someone who was nothing but a memory.

Wyatt turned the car around and headed downtown. There was a parking space open right in front of the ice cream shop. Wyatt parallel parked like a champ.

"Let's get some ice cream!"

The kids both cheered.

"Do you think Uncle Levi is here yet?" Olivia asked, taking Wyatt by the hand as they walked into the shop.

Wyatt didn't see Levi's car outside. He had said something about it not being his night with Isla, so he had to get his ex's permission to take her out. It was possible they'd be a little late. "I don't know—let's have a look around."

That was when he saw *her*. Not Isla. Not Levi. They weren't there yet. Wyatt worried for a second that his mind was playing tricks on him. Was he seeing things because he had been thinking about her so hard? Because that was the only explanation that made sense. Anything else seemed too strange to even consider.

She turned her pretty head in his direction and his knees went weak. Same blond hair, same bottle-green eyes. She was small in stature but anyone who looked at her would have a hard time looking away. Seated at the counter on one of the red padded stools was none other than Miss Harper Hayes.

CHAPTER FOUR

HARPER OPENED HER NOTEBOOK and reviewed her notes. She had jotted down several talking points she wanted to be sure to mention when she finally mustered up the courage to find Wyatt.

"One salted caramel brownie sundae for my favorite customer." Tucker Green was a spry old man with hair as white as the snow that capped the mountains surrounding Eagle Springs. He had a bushy mustache and pale blue eyes. His smile was as contagious as his ice cream was divine.

"I have been thinking about his sundae every day since the last time I ate one." Harper grabbed her phone and took a quick picture of the finished product. Then, with her phone in one hand and her spoon in the other, she took a live photo of her scooping some whipped cream and the cherry off the top. She set the spoon down and worked on adding some embellishments to the photos so she could post them to her social media accounts.

Tucker eyed her curiously. "Are you going to eat it or just take pictures of it?"

She glanced up from her phone. "Oh, trust me, I'm going to eat it. I need before shots so my followers get to see more than an empty bowl." She finished enhancing the photos and turned her full attention to the dessert in front of her. With her eyes closed, Harper hummed as she savored the first bite of ice cream and brownie. "You are a true master of your craft."

Tucker took a bow. "Thank you very much."

Even though this ice cream concoction had more calories than her mother allowed herself in a day, Harper felt no shame and there was no doubt she would have a few more of them before she left Wyoming for good. Right now, if things worked out the way she needed them to, she would be in Eagle Springs for at least a month. Four weeks had to be plenty of time for her to establish she was a happy newlywed.

She was a *newlywed*. Married to a man she didn't even know. A man who probably didn't even realize he was married to her. She took another bite of ice cream. The conversation that she was about to have with Wyatt was destined to be the most awkward one she'd ever had.

"Hey, Tucker," she said, realizing that he might know exactly where she could look for her husband.

Tucker walked back over, buffing a glass bowl with a white towel. "Yes, ma'am?"

"I'm wondering if you can help me find someone. He told me that when he's in town he comes here and you know him well."

"I know a lot of people. Who are you looking for exactly?"

"He claims to be your favorite customer. His name is Wyatt. I don't know his last name. He's tall, broad shoulders, strong arms, dark hair that's kind of wavy but short, and he has this smile that literally makes my heart race in a good way, if you know what I mean."

"I got it." Tucker snickered. "Someone has a crush on Wyatt Blackwell. That's the only Wyatt I know who fits your description."

The relief was instantaneous. "Blackwell! Yes, that was it."

Tucker's expression dampened. "Honestly, I haven't seen Wyatt Blackwell in a while. He's originally from Eagle Springs, but he travels all over the West. I have no idea if he's in town." The bells above the door jangled. "Your best bet would be to head over to the Flying Spur—" Tucker's gaze drifted over Harper's shoulder toward the sound. "Well, well. Goodness almighty, ask and you shall receive."

Harper turned to see what he was staring at only to find it was a who not a what. Wyatt Blackwell was there in the flesh, wide-eyed and frozen in place. Her mouth went dry. She had been working out what to say for days but suddenly felt completely unprepared to have this conversation. He was ruggedly handsome, which was such a cliché but the only way she could think to describe him. It was obvious he spent a lot of time outside; his tanned skin gave that away. She remembered his hands were rough, calloused from the kind of work he did.

She slid off her stool and smoothed out the wrinkles in her shirt. Was there caramel on her face? Why was he staring at her so intently? She wiped at the corner of her mouth to be sure.

"I don't see Uncle Levi," the teenage boy standing beside Wyatt said. "Should we grab a booth? He's probably running late. He does that a lot lately."

"Uh…" Wyatt seemed to snap out of the trance he was in. "Yeah, why don't you two go sit over there." He pointed to an empty corner booth. "I need to say hello to someone. You guys figure out what you want to order while you wait." Slowly, painfully so, he sauntered her way.

"I bet you didn't expect to see me here," she said in an attempt to keep it light. She shrugged and held her palms out. "But, surprise, here I am."

Wyatt narrowed his eyes. There was distrust in his tone. "How did you know I was going to be here?"

Clearly he was concerned that she was some kind of stalker and she couldn't blame him for making that assumption. "I didn't know you were going to be *here* here. I knew you were heading back to Eagle Springs, but I didn't know you'd come get ice cream at the same time as me. It's weird how fate works, isn't it?"

He cocked an eyebrow. "Fate?"

Harper internally cringed. That probably sounded a little bit worrisome. She wasn't here to scare him away with talk of being fated like some kind of romantic fairy tale; she was here to make him a business proposal. They were married and she needed him to play along for a bit, but she had no intention of making this into a real relationship. That would be absurd.

She shook her head. "That's not what I meant. Sorry, I hoped to handle this reunion better than I am."

"Are you in town because of me?"

"Kind of," she replied, probably setting off all kinds of red flags.

"Kind of?"

"Do you remember what happened the night we met?"

"I remember most of it." Wyatt shifted his weight from one leg to the other. "At least I think I do," he added with a bit of uncertainty.

Harper took a deep breath. At least he hadn't run off knowing they were hitched.

That thought had crossed her mind. There had been some fear he had known exactly what they did and took off anyway.

"No judgments," she said. "I don't exactly remember everything either."

"We didn't...you know. I slept on the floor. I woke up on the floor and remember making that decision before anything got out of hand."

"Oh, I know," she assured him. "I am not here because of anything like that. I needed to talk to you about something else."

"You came all the way to Wyoming to talk to me about something? That seems pretty serious. I mean, don't get me wrong, I had a great time with you and your friends, but I don't think we have anything serious enough to come all the way to Wyoming for."

It looked like he wanted to run. She was scaring him away before he even knew why he should actually bolt. She steeled herself for his reaction. "We got married," she blurted out at the same moment the bell above the door jangled.

"Well, well, well, if it isn't my long-lost

baby brother!" a voice boomed, causing Wyatt to turn around.

Another ruggedly handsome cowboy made a beeline for Wyatt and put him in a headlock. The two grown men roughhoused for a couple seconds until the guy shouted something about being careful of his back.

"You are so embarrassing," Wyatt said, giving the man a nudge. He shifted his gaze back to Harper. "You'll have to excuse my brother. He thinks he's still at the rodeo and forgets his manners."

Wyatt's brother picked up his hat and set it back on his head. Grinning from ear to ear, his brother sidled up to her. "Was this man bothering you, miss? Don't let his dimples fool you. He's a love 'em and leave 'em kind of guy. Me, on the other hand…"

Wyatt yanked his brother back and stepped in between them. "Please ignore him. I think you were right about needing to talk, but can I get a minute?"

"Of course," Harper replied, retaking her seat at the counter and using the time to get her heartbeat back under control.

"Who is that?" she heard Wyatt's brother ask as he was led away.

"Nobody you need to know."

Wyatt's reply shouldn't have hurt her feelings, but it did. Harper understood that there was no way they could stay married, but it stung that he didn't want his family to know her at all. There was no reason they couldn't stay friends once this got all cleared up.

Harper glanced over her shoulder at Wyatt, his brother and three kids sitting at the table in the corner. The children were eagerly talking over one another to share all the things they wanted off the menu. The youngest little girl said she couldn't decide. Wyatt seemed to be listening until his gaze met Harper's and it was clear he was distracted by her presence.

His family didn't need to know they were married, but it wouldn't hurt for them to know she existed. There was no reason for her not to introduce herself. She grabbed her sundae and a couple extra napkins and walked over to join their chaos.

"I'm sure you all have been here before, but I have got to recommend the salted caramel brownie sundae."

"Can I get that?" the little girl asked Wyatt.

"You can get anything you want, Olivia."

"Your name is Olivia? That's my middle name."

"Can we get your first name?" Wyatt's brother asked.

"This is Harper," Wyatt said before Harper could answer for herself. "Harper, this is my brother Levi, my nephew Mason, Levi's daughter Isla and my niece Olivia."

Harper smiled. "It's nice to meet all of you."

"Would you like to join us?" Levi asked. "No reason for you to sit over at the counter by yourself. You can sit here right next to me." He asked his daughter to move closer to her cousin and made space for Harper.

"She is not sitting next to you." Wyatt had everyone move the other direction in the semicircular booth. "She can sit right here next to me if she likes," he said, gesturing to the open space.

"Thank you," she said, taking them up on their offer to join.

"Now, can we find out exactly how do you two know each other?" Levi asked.

Wyatt rubbed the back of his neck while Harper took a bite of her sundae. She wasn't answering this question. This was his family. He could explain who they were to each other.

"We, uh, met in Las Vegas actually. Harper won big at the blackjack table."

"What's blackjack?" Olivia asked.

"It's a card game," Mason answered.

"How do you know what blackjack is?" Levi asked. He, like Wyatt, knew Gran did not allow any gambling in the house.

"I'm not a baby. I know about casinos and games like blackjack, poker and crabs."

Levi and Wyatt both laughed at the same time. "I think you mean craps, bud," Wyatt corrected.

Mason's cheeks flushed. Luckily, Tucker came over to take their order, shifting the focus away from his mistake.

The Blackwells began to order their ice cream. When it was Wyatt's turn, Tucker didn't give him a chance to speak. He kept writing and said, "And two scoops of butter pecan on a cake cone for my favorite customer."

Wyatt smiled smugly. "Told you I was his favorite customer. He knows me."

Harper could feel her brows pinch together. "Tucker, you said I was your favorite when you gave me this sundae. Was I your favorite until Wyatt got here? Are we both your favorite? Is everyone your favorite? Inquiring minds need to know."

"Can I be your favorite?" Olivia asked.

"I want to be his favorite." Isla placed her elbows on the table. She clasped her hands together and begged, "Please let me be your favorite. Pleeeeeease."

Everyone stared at Tucker, waiting for him to give them an answer. His grin was wide. "Customers are like ice cream. No one has just one favorite. One day, you want a chocolate milkshake and on another, the only thing you're dreaming about is my amazing banana split with extra whipped cream. Could you possibly say one is your favorite and the other is not? Of course not, you love them all."

Wyatt looked disappointed. "So, we're all your favorite?"

"I wouldn't say that." Tucker put a hand on Levi's shoulder. "I mean, somebody has to be Neapolitan."

It took Levi a second. "Wait, am *I* Neapolitan? No one likes Neapolitan. People *like* me. I was very popular on the circuit."

Wyatt and Harper burst into laughter while the kids sat with confused expressions on their sweet faces. Tucker promised to get their orders made ASAP.

"What's Neapolitan?" Olivia asked.

"It's the ice cream no one orders because it tries too hard to be popular," Wyatt replied, smirking at his brother. Levi flicked Wyatt's hat off his head, but the younger Blackwell took it all in stride. He chuckled as Harper stood up to let him out to get his hat.

Harper never had a brother, but this was what she imagined it would be like. Her mother had been married more times than she could count, but only had one child. Harper had a few stepsiblings over the years. None of them lived with her growing up. Serena tended to marry older men. If they'd had kids from a previous marriage, those children were adults and living anywhere but with their father.

"Bet you're rethinking coming over here to sit with us," Wyatt said to her as they sat back down.

"Your family is just as interesting as you are."

"Who, us?" Levi asked. "This group is only the tip of the Blackwell iceberg. The rest of our family is a lot more than interesting."

"How many brothers and sisters do you have?"

"I have two brothers and two sisters. My oldest sister, Corliss, is married."

"To my dad!" Olivia exclaimed.

"To Olivia's dad, which made Olivia my niece. I now have four nieces and two nephews."

That was a lot more family than Harper had expected. "And you guys all live here in Eagle Springs?"

"We all live here except for this guy." Levi pointed at Wyatt. "He gets a little claustrophobic when he's home."

"Can you blame me? Corliss wanted me to bunk with Mason. No offense, bud."

"I wasn't too excited about rooming with you either. I'm pretty sure sharing a room with an old man wouldn't impress the girls at school."

Wyatt put his hand on his chest. "Old man?"

"You have some girls at school you're

trying to impress? Does your mother know about this?" Levi asked.

"I do not talk to my mom about my love life," the teenager replied.

"Your love life?" both men said at the same time.

Tucker saved Mason's day by returning to the table with their ice cream. The girls didn't wait to dive in. It took three seconds for Olivia to have ice cream on her chin and whipped cream on the tip of her nose. Wyatt tried to get her to stop eating long enough to wipe it off. Isla and her dad traded bites. Mason took a picture of his sundae like a true social media expert.

For that moment, Harper let herself feel what it would be like to be part of a real family. Legally, she was truly part of this one. At least until the annulment papers were filed. Would he tell his family what actually happened? Would he agree to go along with her social media ruse and have to lie to his family about being happily married for the next month? Would he not even tell them, cover it all up?

Wyatt nudged her gently with his elbow. "Your ice cream is melting."

She'd been so distracted by their playful interactions that she forgot to eat her own sundae. She gave him a smile as she picked up her spoon and took another bite. The next four weeks were going to be even more interesting than this family turned out to be.

"If I treat, can you give the kids a ride back to the ranch?" Wyatt asked Levi as he pulled out his wallet and set some money on the table. "I need to talk to Harper before I head back."

Levi raised his eyebrows but didn't say a word about Wyatt's request. "Everyone thank Uncle Wyatt for the ice cream and then let's head out!"

"Thank you, Uncle Wyatt!" the three kids said in unison.

"You're welcome."

Levi got to his feet. "Harper, it was nice to meet you. Hopefully, we will get the *real* story about how you two met and why you are here visiting my brother in our little town many, many miles away from Las Vegas."

"It was nice to meet you, too. Hopefully, we'll meet again and swap Wyatt stories."

"Oh, I like this one. I like this one a lot. I've got stories. So many stories that will

only be shared if the sharing is recipro-
cated."

"Bye now," Wyatt said gruffly.

The kids said their goodbyes and followed
Levi out the door. Harper stood up.

"I thought we were going to talk."

"Oh, we are." He slid out of the booth
and held out his hand. "Just not here. Small
towns have big ears. We'll be lucky if no one
heard what you said to me earlier. I'm praying you said it so fast that no one caught it
or I misheard you. I've been praying for that
this whole time."

Harper took his hand, grabbed her bag
and went out with him. She had hoped that
he might be slightly amused by this whole
debacle. Wyatt didn't seem to find any of
this very funny.

"I don't think you misheard me," she said
as he led her outside and let go of her hand.

"I was afraid you were going to say that.
Follow me." He picked up the pace as they
walked down the sidewalk and around the
corner. Harper had to jog a bit to keep up.
Wyatt didn't slow down until they passed
a sign that said Eagle Springs Elementary.

He guided her toward the small playground behind the small brick building.

Wyatt surveyed the area, making sure no one was nearby. She wasn't sure how to break it to him that she needed people to see them together. That was why she was there.

"What happened that night?" He sat down on one of the swings and took off his hat. He stared inside it like he was going to find some answers in there.

Harper gripped the chains on the swing next to him. The metal was cold and her hands were sweaty. "I woke up the other morning and all I could remember was that I had met this really cute guy and won some money playing cards. When my friends came to check on me, they showed me some pictures I posted online. There was also a video."

She pulled up the post and found the video before handing him the phone. Wyatt watched as they were pronounced husband and wife by a man dressed in costume.

"We really got married? How can that be legal when we were clearly not of sound mind?"

Harper sat on the swing and used her feet

to push her forward and back. "I don't know, but my lawyer said that it will be easy to annul because of that."

"Okay, good. What do I have to do? Do I need a lawyer?"

Proposition time. Harper needed to make her case for staying married. "You don't need a lawyer. I already had mine draw up the decree we both sign and send to the court."

"Great!" Wyatt brightened and set his hat back on his head. "I'll sign. No problem."

"Well, actually there's a tiny problem," she said, twisting her swing so she was facing him. "That post was seen by most of my followers. It has already been liked by over two million people."

Wyatt's eyes nearly bugged out of his head. "Two million people?"

"Remember when I told you I was kind of famous? I wasn't kidding. I have a very large following on the internet. They listen to me when I tell them where to vacation, what to buy their girlfriend for Christmas, what to order at my favorite restaurants all over the country, all over the world in fact."

"Two million people. You know two million people?"

"No, that's not how it works. I have followers who live everywhere. There's only a few people on my account who I know offline."

"Okay, so most of these people are strangers. Who cares if they know we got married in Vegas after a few too many drinks at the bar?"

"My reputation online is what pays my bills. I can't break trust with my followers or they will unfollow me. If they unfollow me, they don't read my posts. If they don't read my posts, I don't get paid by my sponsors and advertisers."

Wyatt's brow furrowed. "So what are you saying?"

"I plan to sign the papers. I do. And I want you to sign the papers. *Eventually*. But I need your help to end this in a way that doesn't make me look bad in front of all of these followers."

"Won't signing the papers end this? What else do you need me to do?"

"I need you to pretend to be married to me until I can bail out gracefully."

"Pretend to be married? You just said you don't even know any of these people who follow you. I can also assure you that none of your followers are hanging around here in Eagle Springs. Things on the internet take a backseat to all the things right in front of you around here. Why would we need to pretend to be married?"

Harper exhaled sharply. She wasn't doing a very good job explaining to this cowboy how the world of social media worked.

"It doesn't matter what people here in Eagle Springs think. For all I care, you can tell everyone you know that I am just a friend you met while you were out of town. I just need you to let me hang out with you, take some pictures, let me post some things on the internet. All you have to do is have some fun with me for a few weeks."

"Are you serious?" Wyatt nearly fell out of his swing. He stood up and began to pace around. "This sounds like a bad idea. Like I told you before, Harper. I think you are a very nice person. I wish you nothing but the best, but I am here to work on my family's ranch. I am pretty much the only one who will be working on my family's ranch for the foreseeable future. I don't have time for things like fun and hanging out."

"I get it. I know you have a life. I'm not here to make it harder, but my life, my livelihood depends on me saving face here. I can't be the woman who gets married drunk and has to turn around and get divorced a few days later. It's not who my followers think I am."

Wyatt jammed his hands on his hips. "It is who you are, though. That's what happened. Wouldn't it be better to be honest about what went down? Wouldn't that be what your followers expect from you?"

Harper stood up and kicked some mulch. Being honest was tempting, but dangerous. "I know it seems simple. I wish it was."

Her phone rang in her hand. It was her mom's husband. He had dropped her off at Tucker's while he took care of some business in town.

"I have to answer this. Hold on," she said. Wyatt motioned for her to go ahead. "Hello?"

"Where are you? I'm parked outside Tucker's and I don't see you in there."

"Sorry, I'm just around the corner. I'll be there in a few minutes."

"What does that mean? Why are you wandering around? I need to get back to the house."

Harper hadn't explained to her mother what she was doing in town. She certainly hadn't filled in Stepdad of the Moment. "I'm over by the elementary school. Just wait for me by Tucker's. I'll be there in a minute." She hung up and turned her attention back to Wyatt. "My mom's husband is waiting for me. I know that I've shocked you. Maybe we should get a good night's sleep and talk again tomorrow. Can I give you my phone number?"

"Let me give you mine," he said. He rattled off his number and she typed it into her contacts. "I'm up before the sun and working all day. I'm not going to be available until the evening."

"So I shouldn't take offense if you don't respond to my text right away?"

"I'm not real good with that texting stuff. You're better off calling me."

"I think you are the first person under the age of fifty to say those words."

He stared at her curiously.

A car horn honked. "Harper! Let's go!"

Wyatt's eyes narrowed. "Is that Brock Bedford?"

Harper hadn't been this embarrassed since the time she was fifteen and one of her mother's other husbands answered the door in nothing but bathing suit briefs when her friends came over.

"Sorry. Yeah, that's Brock. Thanks to an Alaskan cruise they both decided to take a year ago, I have another stepfather to bond with. Apparently this one is more impatient than I realized."

Wyatt scrubbed his face with his hand. "You cannot tell him how you know me. We need to sign those papers, Harper. We need to sign them immediately."

CHAPTER FIVE

THERE WERE TWO THINGS Gran valued above all others—hard work and loyalty. Wyatt was as hardworking as they came and his grandmother would agree. She did, however, take issue with the fact that he didn't choose to do that work on the family ranch. She didn't try to stop him when he told her how he wanted to live his life, but she didn't hide the fact that she felt somewhat abandoned. Her hardworking grandson didn't want to work hard for her. Sometimes that made him wonder if she considered him disloyal.

Wyatt wouldn't have to wonder what she thought if she found out that he had married the stepdaughter of the person she currently hated the most in this world. It was bad enough that he went to Vegas and somehow ended up married to anyone, but to be married to someone related to Brock Bedford? Disastrous.

Given the fact that Gran sort of attacked him not too long ago and was arrested at the bank, it was also highly likely that Brock wouldn't be too happy about his stepdaughter being married to a Blackwell. That was why Wyatt took off from the park before Brock recognized it was him talking to Harper.

Wyatt's whole body was humming with nervous energy. He needed Harper to give him those annulment papers so he could sign them and pretend this never happened. He didn't really care what her "followers" thought about it. This mess needed to be cleaned up fast.

Levi's truck was parked in front of the house when Wyatt made it home. There was no telling what he had told the rest of the family about their surprise guest at the ice cream shop. Wyatt was only dropping by the house to do a little damage control.

"I've got Molly looking into it," Levi said when Wyatt stepped into the dining room. Corliss, Nash, Gran and Levi were all sitting at the table.

Corliss was the first to notice the new arrival. "Look who's home."

All eyes shifted to Wyatt. "Did you win big in Vegas and not tell us?" Nash asked.

"No, why?"

"Levi tells us some beautiful woman followed you all the way to Eagle Springs after meeting you in Sin City. The only reason that would happen is she saw you hit the jackpot," Nash hypothesized.

Levi and Nash had a good laugh. Corliss kept staring at him like she actually believed that might be true and desperately needed him to confirm or deny it.

"You guys are hilarious. You think I would have come here to work if I had a million-dollar jackpot to pay the mortgage off?"

"So then what was that about? You want me to believe that you met someone in Vegas and a couple days later she just happened to show up in Eagle Springs?" Levi cocked his head to the side waiting for an answer.

"Her mom lives in Eagle Springs, doofus. Her being here doesn't have anything to do with me. It's just a small world." Too small if they asked Wyatt.

"Who's her mom?" Gran asked, tossing her long gray braid over her shoulder. Denny

Blackwell knew everyone in town. It probably bothered her when Levi said they had ice cream with someone named Harper and she didn't know who he was talking about.

Thankfully, Wyatt didn't know who her mom was, only her stepdad. It was helpful to not have to lie. "I have no idea. I never asked because it didn't seem important."

"You guys going to hang out while she's in town? She seems to like you. This might be your big chance, little brother," Levi teased.

"You're the only one of us who hasn't even attempted to settle down," Corliss chimed in. "Maybe the universe is trying to tell you something by putting you and this woman in the same place twice."

"Yeah, I don't know about that," Wyatt said. "She won't be in town very long. I doubt I'll even see her again while she's here."

"I'm not sure any of us should be giving our baby brother advice about settling down," Nash reminded them all. "It's not like we've all been very successful at it."

He wasn't wrong about that. All of Wyatt's siblings had some trouble in that area. Corliss had been left at the altar during her first attempt at settling down. Nash and Levi were divorced. Adele was widowed with two kids just like their grandmother had been. Gran had raised her family alone after being widowed when she was pregnant with Wyatt's dad and uncle. Other than their mom and dad, the Blackwells did not have the best track record with long-term relationships. It was probably one of the reasons he avoided serious relationships like the plague.

"He wouldn't be a Blackwell if he didn't have one failed marriage," Levi joked.

Great, he'd managed to cross that off this sad Blackwell bucket list. He just wasn't about to tell his family that, though. "Again, I am glad I could amuse you four this evening. I am going to go get ready for bed so I can fall asleep as soon as the sun goes down. I have to be up early in the morning. Corliss has another list for me, I'm sure."

She smiled. "You know it."

"That's it?" Levi complained. "I thought we were going to get all the details about this woman and why you had to talk to her alone. Uh oh, are you hiding something? Are you keeping a big secret from us? Is someone going to be a…daddy?"

"Now that makes sense," Nash said with a nod.

Corliss shook her head. "You guys are too much. You don't get pregnant and two days later have a positive pregnancy test. That's not how it works. You both have children. How can you not know that?"

"I was just joking, gosh," Levi said in his defense. "I knew there was no way she was pregnant. That woman was way out of Wyatt's league."

"All right, that's enough," Gran said, losing her patience. "Why don't you tell me what else you're planning with the rodeo."

That was Wyatt's cue to hightail it to Betty. He went outside and went to grab some stuff out of his truck when a car he didn't recognize came flying down the drive. It pulled up right behind him.

Harper jumped out. "Oh, good. I found you."

How had she gotten here so fast? Wyatt glanced up at the house to make sure no one had followed him out. When the coast was clear, he tried to stop her from getting too far from her car. "Did you bring the papers? We can sign them in the car."

"I don't have the papers. I need you to hear me out about this."

"There is nothing to hear." He lowered his voice as he checked again over his shoulder to make sure no one came out of the house as the dogs started barking from inside. They must have noticed there was a visitor. He needed to get Harper out of here. "I want an annulment. You want an annulment. We should get an annulment."

"I have a brand to protect. That probably doesn't make a lot of sense to you since my world and your world are very different. I wouldn't have come all the way to Wyoming to ask you to do this for me if I didn't think this was important. Please, Wyatt. You have to help me."

Why did she want to make this so hard? This conversation was clearly going to last longer than Wyatt could risk. Bow and Arrow were loud. "Can you drive me to my trailer? Come on—it's just down this road." He opened her car door so she could get back inside.

Her forehead creased with confusion. "Oh…okay."

He hustled over to the passenger side and

climbed in. "I don't stay in the main house. We've got a full house these days. My sister just got married and they have Mason and Olivia, who you met. My older brother also lives here. Then there's my grandma and we've got two dogs. Like I said, full house."

"Gotcha."

"Plus I like my privacy. I am a private person."

Harper nodded and followed his directions toward the empty bunkhouse. "Who stays here?" she asked.

"Usually the guys we hire to work on the ranch, but right now, I am the only one they can afford."

"Why aren't you staying in there then?"

Wyatt got out of the car and waited for her to join him. "I use the bathroom and such in there, but Betty is my home. I prefer to be in my space."

"Betty is your camper?"

"She is." He gave Betty a pat.

Harper sighed with relief. "Betty is a camper. I remembered you saying something about going back to Wyoming with Betty. I assumed it was a person, not a thing."

"Oh, so you thought I not only married you but was going home with another woman?"

"She also could have been a dog. That was my other guess."

"Ah, yes. The dog that I brought to Vegas with me but left alone all day and night."

"Like I said, the truth makes a lot more sense."

The truth. He liked the truth. The truth would set them free. "We need to sign the papers, Harper. I know you have people who think this is a real relationship, but it's going to hurt less if we are honest with them. I promise."

Harper ducked her head before looking back up at him. "I understand why you think that. I do. I don't want to make your life more complicated. I just need you to delay signing the papers and let me post some pictures of us together."

She was right; he did not understand. How did someone make a living by taking pictures of themselves? And why did it matter if he was in those pictures or not? "Listen, I'm sorry this is bad for your business, but staying together would be bad for my business. I am going to be working all day, every day. There isn't going to be time for us to hang out. Not to mention, your stepdad and my grandmother are not exactly each other's biggest fan."

"Your family knows Brock?"

"Small town, remember? Everyone knows everyone for the most part. Not to mention my grandmother is very popular in these parts and Brock has quite the reputation as well."

"No one here in Eagle Springs has to know. I won't say anything to my mom or Brock. You don't have to tell your family. We can just be friends. It's not a big deal to be friends with Brock's stepdaughter, is it?"

She was relentless and beautiful. He hated that this attraction clouded his thinking. Wyatt was torn. It would not go over well with the family if they learned the truth. "I don't know, Harper."

"Do you think anyone in your circle follows me on the internet?"

"Absolutely not. None of them."

"I'm positive that my family doesn't either. We can do this," she assured him. "I promise you, once enough time has passed, we'll sign and it will all be over."

The Blackwells didn't spend time on social media. They had too much to do every day to spend time on their phones or computers. It wasn't as if they would somehow stumble upon some random influencer.

He couldn't believe he was actually considering this. "How long? I need a specific amount of time. A clear end."

Her face lit up. It was frustratingly satisfying. Making her happy better not come back to bite him.

"Give me until the end of the month. I will do all of the work. I just need you to look cute. That shouldn't be too hard, right?"

A whole month? An uneasy feeling settled in his stomach. "We sign and file the papers on the last day of the month. No take backs."

"No take backs." Her smile was big and bright. She was over the moon and it scared him to death. "Can we take a picture to make this deal official? I think my followers would love to meet Betty."

She took out her phone and wrapped an arm around his waist. As if this situation wasn't awkward enough, now he was going to have to pose for pictures. Wyatt didn't take selfies. That wasn't a thing in his world.

He readjusted his hat and let her settle in against him. Her hair smelled like flowers. He had to stop himself from dipping his head to get the full effect.

"All you have to do is smile, Cowboy Wyatt. Everyone already loves you."

He wasn't sure he wanted "everyone" to love him. Wyatt valued his privacy and enjoyed keeping his circle of friends small. Whenever he felt like he was getting too close to others, he moved on. That was the way he preferred it. He couldn't leave home. Not right now when his family needed him. That meant if Harper stuck around, he was stuck with her. He couldn't forget that this would be over at the end of the month. They couldn't possibly get attached before then.

"Smile," she repeated as she held her phone out.

Wyatt stared at the image of the two of them on her screen. This better not be a mistake. He faked a smile.

Harper dropped her arm and scowled up at him. "Oh my gosh, you look like I'm torturing you. Pretend you just hit blackjack or did a really cool ranching thing."

That actually made him smile. "A cool ranching thing?"

"Yeah," she said, holding her phone back up. "I don't know what ranchers do, but there's got to be something cool that makes you smile." She snapped a couple pictures.

"The only true part of that sentence is you do not know what ranchers do."

"Well, I am excited that you are going to teach me." She took another picture of Wyatt's shocked face. "That is hilarious." She reviewed her photos.

"What do you mean by I am going to teach you about ranching?"

"If you're working all the time, the only way I'm going to get to spend time with you is if I do some work with you," she said as if that was a perfectly reasonable thing to say.

Wyatt shook his head. "You are not working with me."

"Why not?"

"Because you have no idea what you're doing and having you around would just make things take longer than they should."

Harper put her hands on her hips. "I will have you know that I am a very fast learner.

I also love a challenge. Do not underestimate me."

She was feisty. He'd give her that much. "I'm not trying to offend you. I'm only trying to be clear about how important it is for me to be efficient. I can't afford distractions."

"I will not be a distraction. I am good at reading situations. If it seems like I'm in the way, I will get out of the way. I swear." She held her hand up like she was in court with the other hand on a Bible.

"Brief visits. You take your pictures and then you're on your merry way. Deal?"

"Fine," she relented. "But if you have so much work to do, I would think you'd welcome a little assistance. I'm very assistant-y."

Wyatt tried and failed not to laugh. She had been very entertaining since he'd met her, but offering to help was a different story. "I really need to hit the hay. Call me before you come over. I need a heads-up. Always."

"Right. Of course." Her attention was quickly stolen by the sky behind him. "Wow. The sunsets out here are gorgeous."

The sky was an array of colors. Oranges and reds filled the horizon while the clouds above had turned purple and pink. Shades of blue lingered up high.

Harper's phone was out again as she took more pictures. "This really is beautiful country."

Wyatt tried to focus on the sky, but the way the setting sun cast this glow across her face, he couldn't look away. He had enjoyed what he could recall about that night in Vegas more than he should have.

"You should get going. There aren't nearly as many streetlights in Eagle Springs as there are in Las Vegas. Everything always looks different in the dark."

She was quiet, studying him before she said, "Thanks for looking out for me. I'll call you tomorrow."

"Good night, Harper."

"Sleep well, Cowboy Wyatt," she said, backing away.

She had his mind whirling, which meant that things were not going to be easy. Harper was going to call him and then she was going to show up back here and he was going to have to find a way to explain why she was there to his family. His life had suddenly become more complicated than ever before.

CHAPTER SIX

HARPER COULDN'T STOP looking at the photos she had taken at the Flying Spur. Wyatt had agreed to her proposal and let her set the stage for their fake happy honeymoon. That's what she was calling this excursion to Wyoming—their honeymoon. People would buy that.

"What are you busy working on? Selling people some new face cream or something?" Brock asked as he poured himself a cup of coffee. Her new stepdad had a long face and a well-groomed beard and mustache. He had the kind of build that made her believe he was, at one time, an athletic guy. The roundness of his belly told her he hadn't kept up with his former exercise routine.

Harper shut her laptop. She had set herself up in the kitchen because it was the last place in the house her mother would ever linger. Serena wasn't a big fan of cooking. She didn't care for any of the domestic chores that came with living in a house. That was what she had housekeepers, dry cleaners, and restaurants for.

"I've been focusing more on travel lately. Wyoming has the potential to become a popular destination."

"Oh, really?" Brock blew on his coffee. "What do you know about it?"

"I know that Bozeman, Montana, has been nicknamed Boz Angeles because it's been attracting a lot of the Hollywood types. Wyoming and Montana aren't that much different."

Brock raised an eyebrow, his curiosity piqued. "Boz Angeles?"

"That's what they call it. I've had people suggest I do a series on the resorts there. I've been trying to decide if I want to go in the summer and stay at a guest ranch or go in the winter and treat it more like Aspen."

"You really know about this stuff," he said, sounding a bit too astounded.

"This is how I make a living. If I want to go to Bozeman, I'll stay for free and, depending on when I go, I'll get companies to sponsor my outings and adventures."

Brock joined her at the kitchen table. "How do you do that?"

Clearly her mother did not talk to her husband about what she did. Maybe Serena didn't even realize how many connections or how much influence Harper had.

"I partner with various companies all the time. If I'm going for a week of skiing, I'll get in touch with companies that sell ski gear, outdoor clothing and maybe even somebody who sells cute sunglasses or fun hats and mittens."

"And why would they give you their stuff?"

"Because I have a huge following online and if I post about being somewhere, wearing something, doing some activity, people listen and they buy those things or go to those places as well."

"Why have you never told me about this before?"

Harper shrugged. "You never asked."

"When you say you have a huge following, what are we talking about?"

"Millions of followers on every social media platform you can think of."

Brock shouldn't have taken a sip of his coffee at the same time she said the word *millions*. He nearly choked. Harper got up and patted him on the back until he waved her off.

"I'm good, I'm good. You have millions of followers? And these companies you partner with pay you and give you free stuff?"

"That's how it works."

"Fascinating." He smoothed down his tie. "I know some people planning big things here in Eagle Springs. I wonder what they'd say if I brought you aboard. You could make me a valued member of the team."

"You have a team?"

"I'm working on it. I've scratched their backs, hoping they'll scratch mine. The more I can do for them, the more they'll do for me. We should talk again. I'd love to hear your thoughts on the ideas I know they've been throwing around."

Was Brock offering her a job? It was actually kind of nice to have someone recognize the value she could bring to a situation. Her mom never seemed to notice or think too much of what she did. Last night, she had to work overtime to convince Wyatt that her career was real and was important.

"I'd love to talk things over with you," she

said, happy to be appreciated. "Sounds like you're getting in right from the start. That's a good place to be."

"I think this could be huge. It's going to help me make a real name for myself here in Eagle Springs. Your mom is going to love it, and it could make me filthy rich."

"Did someone say filthy rich?" Harper's mom glided into the kitchen. Leave it to Serena to show her face when the conversation turned to money. "Can you get me some coffee, sweetheart?" she asked Brock, taking a seat at the table instead of walking five steps over to the counter where the coffee maker was sitting. "What are you two talking about?"

Brock must have been completely smitten because he jumped right up and poured her a mug. "I've been hearing about your daughter's business connections. I didn't realize she had such marketing power."

He added some sugar, cream and a squirt of vanilla syrup before serving her. Serena kissed his cheek and blew on her drink. She tapped her deep red manicured nails against the mug. "Oh, and here I thought that business degree I paid for was only good at making her famous on social media."

Sometimes her mother acted as if Harper's job wasn't real because she was self-employed and not working a nine-to-five job for some boring company.

"You sure weren't complaining that my being famous on social media wasn't good enough when I gave you those four designer handbags or when I invited you along on that all-expenses paid trip to Maui."

"I do love that one clutch you gave me," her mom said, setting her coffee back on the table. "But getting free stuff from people because you're young and adorable isn't going to pay the bills later. Not unless that fame helps you hook an even more famous man with money to burn."

Serena's answer to all of life's problems was to marry someone wealthy. She'd done it time and time again. Unfortunately, not marrying for love tended to end in divorce. Harper wanted to kick herself for signing a marriage license. It was something she had sworn she'd never do. She did not need a man to take care of her. Harper was capa-

ble of making her own money and support-
ing herself.

"It's a good thing that I do more than look
pretty."

"I think I'm going to mention that she's
here in town to Mr. Howard," Brock told
Serena. "This could be huge for us."

"I like the sound of that. Mama needs a
new Mercedes." Harper's mom puckered up.

Brock leaned down and planted a kiss on
her lips. "Mama is going to get a new Mercedes and anything else she wants."

Harper was about to throw up the toast
she'd had for breakfast. She got up from the
table and grabbed her laptop. "Speaking of
cars, can I borrow one today? I need to run
a couple errands."

"Why don't we go together? You know
there's no one who loves to shop as much
as I do," her mother replied.

There was no way she could bring her
mother with her to visit Wyatt. Neither one
of these two could know she was involved
with a Blackwell. She wished she had rented
a car at the airport instead of letting Brock
pick her up.

"I'm not shopping. I have work to do.

You would be completely bored out of your mind."

"Oh." Serena's face fell. "Can we get lunch later?"

"Probably. I should be done by then. I'll text you."

"I need to eat by noon or I get light-headed. That means we need to be seated somewhere by eleven forty-five. You can't leave me stranded here without a car. I'll pass out."

The woman had so little to do in her day-to-day life, she had to make lunch a huge production. It wasn't like there wasn't food in the house, but Harper knew better than to suggest she make herself a sandwich. "Fine. I'll be sure to get back in time to take you to lunch."

"Thank you. Come give me a good-morning hug. I've missed you. I'm so glad you came to visit."

Harper set her laptop down on the island and gave her mom a hug. Serena wasn't perfect. She definitely had her flaws, but she loved Harper and had done what she could to give her daughter the best of everything.

"I'm glad I came to visit, too. I'm looking forward to lunch with you."

"There's this super cute Italian bake shop downtown. You'll love it. The woman who runs it makes everything herself. She starts baking bread at five every morning. They have a pear-and-walnut salad that's to die for."

"An Italian bake shop in the middle of Wyoming, huh?" Maybe this town had a surprise or two up its sleeve.

"It's your kind of place. You'll want to post about it on your pages for sure."

Harper gave her mom one more squeeze. "I'm sure I will."

First, she needed to get pictures of herself playing the doting wife to her rancher husband. Maybe she could find a big hay bale to pose in front of or a horse to feed a carrot to today. Harper definitely needed to do research on what makes people want to spend a week at a dude ranch.

Harper retreated to the guest bedroom they had her sleeping in. It was the most feminine room in the house. Apparently, this room was where Brock's mother used to stay when she would come visit him. He had shared that the quilt on the bed was hand-made by her. It was beautiful, but not exactly Harper's style. Mrs. Bedford had been a big fan of roses and pastels. She also loved doi-lies. Harper guessed his mom also crocheted those as well.

Once safely in her room, she called Wy-att's number. It rang and rang until his voice mail picked up. There was no personalized message; he simply used the robot voice that read back the number and told you to leave a message.

"Hey, Wyatt. This is Harper. You prob-ably know that. Phones tell you who's call-ing but only if you added me as a contact. Maybe you do, but if you don't then now you know it's me." She sat down on the bed and internally pleaded with herself to stop talking. The voice mail gods actually put her out of her misery.

"Press one if you'd like to listen to your message before sending. Press two if you'd like to record a new message—"

"Two, two, two, please two." Harper hit the button and waited for a second chance to leave a message.

"Your message has been sent. Thank you."

"No! I hit two! I hit two!"

She looked down at her screen. In her haste to hit the number two, she had inadvertently hit the number three. Wyatt was going to listen to the most embarrassing message she'd ever left anyone in her life. She had to call back because she had told him nothing other than she was awful at leaving messages.

She dialed again. "Keep it short and sweet. Don't ramble. Be cool."

"Hello?" Wyatt answered.

Harper was unprepared for him to answer the phone. She was ready to leave a short and sweet message. Her mouth was sealed shut. She couldn't speak.

"Hello?" He sounded irritated. He was going to think she was some spam caller and never answer her calls again.

"Hey! Harper." She pinched the bridge of her nose. Since when did a guy make her so tongue-tied? She couldn't even spit out a full sentence.

"Harper?"

"Yeah, this is Harper. Hi. I wasn't expecting you to pick up. I called a second ago and got your voice mail, so I assumed you would let it go to voice mail again, but you picked up. I didn't think you would. I'm glad you did, though. I wanted to talk to you not your voice mail." Great, her mouth worked again but it was back to only being capable of rambling.

"Are you okay?" Concern etched his tone.

Harper took a deep breath. She needed to pull herself together. "Sorry. I think I had one too many cups of coffee this morning. I was calling to see if I could stop by. I promise I won't stay long."

Concern shifted back to annoyance. "I have a very long list of things to do today. I'm not sure it's best for your picture-taking thing."

"I know you're worried I'm going to get in the way and I promise, I won't. I will be in and out so fast, you'll feel like you didn't even see me." *Please, please, please let me come.*

She could hear Wyatt sigh long and hard on the other end of the line. "Can you come during my lunch break?"

"What time do you take lunch?" She couldn't not go to lunch with her mom.

"Right at noon."

"Perfect." If Serena needed to eat before noon, she could definitely eat earlier. They would eat, Harper could drop off her mom back at home and she could easily be at the Blackwell ranch by noon. "I'll bring you something to eat."

"You don't have to do that."

"I want to do it. Let me do something for you since you're doing something for me." Hopefully ranchers liked Italian bake shop food.

"I'll see you at noon. Meet me by Betty."

"Thank you. I'll see you then." This would work. Harper would make this work.

"CAN I GET you ladies anything else?" Marie Piccoli asked when she stopped by Harper and Serena's table. She was the owner of Marie's Italian Bake Shop, an adorable little café that immediately transported Harper to a town in Italy. It was an unexpected treat in the middle of a traditionally Western area.

Marie was a dainty woman probably in her fifties. She had jet-black hair and loved her rouge. Harper wanted so badly to pull up a chair and learn more about her. What brought her to Eagle Springs, Wyoming and what made her stay? There had to be a story behind it.

"We have to split one of those cannoli. You won't regret it, Harper."

"They are my favorite thing to eat here, too," Marie said with a wink as she jotted it down.

"Could I get something to go as well?" Harper asked before she left. "I'd like an order of your nonna's lasagna."

Her mother gasped. "When in the world are you going to eat all those carbs?"

"Like you said, this place is perfect for me to post about. I want to try a few different dishes. Plus, I am not scared of a few carbs. Don't worry about me, Mom."

Serena sighed. "I miss being young and having a functioning metabolism."

Harper's mom was too hard on herself. She was hyperfocused on how she looked because that was how she measured her worth as a person. She was gorgeous and being beautiful had served her well over the years. However, as she got older, the fear that she wouldn't always be the prettiest one in the room started to take root. Harper learned from her mother's mistakes and sought to define herself as more than a pretty face.

Serena wasn't afraid of carbs when they came in the form of delicious cannoli. The one brought to their table had a shell dipped in chocolate and filled with sweet ricotta and mini chocolate chips. The ends of the cannoli were covered in chopped pistachios that added that hint of salt. Harper had her mother pose for a picture holding the delectable treat.

"Make sure you tell your followers we split this."

Harper laughed. "Heaven forbid the world thinks you ate a whole cannoli. They might believe you…enjoy good food." She fake gasped.

Her mother was unamused. "Just for that, you get the smaller half."

"I'll be sure to add that detail to the post," Harper teased. Her mom threw her napkin at her and Harper laughed harder.

To make up for giving Serena such a hard time, she snatched up the bill and paid for her mom and, secretly, Wyatt's lunch. Ranchers probably liked pasta. It was good, stick-to-your-ribs food. That seemed like the kind of stuff a hardworking guy would eat.

"I have two episodes of our favorite reality TV show saved on my DVR. Will you come watch with me?" Serena asked as they got in the car.

"I need to run those errands I was going to take care of earlier, but we can watch when I get home. I shouldn't be long. I have a very strict time frame to work with."

Serena gazed out the window with a frown on her face. "Fine. I'll only watch one episode and save the second one for us to watch together. There isn't much else for me to do when Brock is at work."

"You need to make some friends around here. There have to be women who enjoy playing golf or maybe mah-jongg. You loved that back in LA."

Serena shrugged. "There are no golf courses in Eagle Springs. I don't even know if there is one within a hundred miles of this place. And most of the women around here seem to work and wear plaid. They do things like ride horses. I am not learning to ride a horse."

This was one of Harper's big fears when

her mom said she was moving to Wyoming. Harper knew Serena would be a fish out of water in a town like this. That didn't bode well for Serena and Brock's marriage. If Serena got too isolated, she would bolt. She was good at that.

"They can't all ride horses and live on ranches. What about Marie? Maybe you and she could be friends."

"The bake shop lady? What in the world would we have in common? She makes bread from scratch. I can barely make toast without burning it."

That was no lie. Harper suppressed a laugh. "You both have been to Italy. She is obviously from there and you have visited a few times. You share a love of her cannoli. Imagine if you started hanging out and she brought you a whole box of them to munch on."

Serena glared at her daughter from the passenger's seat. "You want me to gain ten pounds, don't you?"

"You are beautiful, Mom. Even if you gained ten pounds, you'd still be beautiful."

"You're the only one who believes that," her mom scoffed.

Harper decided right then that she would spend the next few weeks not only protecting her image online but also finding her mom a way to connect with her new surroundings and neighbors. Serena wouldn't do it on her own and Harper didn't want to see her mom divorced yet again. There was only going to be one divorce coming out of Eagle Springs…just as soon as she convinced her followers that she was happily married.

After dropping Serena back at the house, Harper headed over to the Blackwell ranch. The Flying Spur was one of the largest ranches in Eagle Springs. Harper had done some research on the Blackwells since she'd last been here. Denny Blackwell, Wyatt's grandmother, was kind of a big deal in these parts. The Flying Spur trained horses, some of which had been sold to riders who had won big at the local rodeos.

Harper had never been to a rodeo, but her interest had been piqued. Turned out that Wyatt's brother Levi, the guy from the ice cream shop, had been somewhat of a hot-shot in the rodeo world. The article she read about him said he had recently suffered a career-ending injury.

Wyatt was sitting outside Betty in a camping chair drinking from an old metal thermos when she pulled up. He got to his feet as soon as she parked her car.

"I hope you're hungry." Harper held up her take-out container. "Marie made this especially for you."

"Marie?"

"From Marie's Italian Bake Shop. You have to know the place. It's on Forest Avenue. It's close to that little art studio."

"Art studio?" Wyatt took the container from her and popped it open. "Oh my goodness, this smells darn good."

"Marie makes all her pasta by hand. If you really haven't been there, you need to check it out."

He invited her inside and pulled two forks from a drawer. "Did you bring something to eat or are we sharing?"

"Sorry, I ate with my mom. I know you wanted me out of your hair quickly. I figured you could eat and I could take some pictures. I saw that field on my way in with all those hay bales—would it be okay if I took some pictures out there?"

Wyatt had sat down at his dining table with a mouthful of food. He held up a finger while he chewed. When he finally swallowed, he explained, "You can't roam around the property without me. If my sister found you hanging out in one of our pastures by yourself, she'd wonder what was going on."

"Oh, okay. I'll wait for you to finish eating then." Harper sat down across from him on the dusky-blue banquet seat.

Betty wasn't very big. There was seating for four people and a dinette table at one end and what looked like a full-size bed on the other. Directly across from where you entered was the kitchen, which consisted of the smallest sink Harper had ever seen, two gas burners, a mini fridge and a microwave. Wyatt's clothes were spilling out of the tiny closet that was situated next to the bed and opposite that was what Harper assumed was the bathroom. No wonder Wyatt used the facilities in the bunkhouse. It didn't look like someone Wyatt's size could even fit in there.

Being inside Betty allowed her to get a glimpse at who Wyatt was. He was fairly tidy, maybe because there was nowhere to leave anything out. He was definitely a minimalist. There was a small plant sitting next to the sink, however. It warmed her heart that he put forth effort to keep something alive. When she added the fact that the man took his nieces and nephew out for ice cream the other day, it was hard not to be a little smitten.

Wyatt had gotten right back to shoveling lasagna into that mouth of his. When he came up for air, he wiped the sides of his mouth with a napkin. "There's an art studio in town?"

"One that offers classes for kids and Tuesday night wine-and-paint parties for the moms. I'm sure dads are welcome, too."

He shook his head. "Never heard of it. Maybe it's new. I haven't been home in a while."

Hillshire Art looked like it had been there forever, but maybe they just wanted it to seem that way. Wyatt had to know this town better than she did. "Maybe one Tuesday night we could go get a bottle of wine and paint something together."

Wyatt stared at her like she had asked him

to climb Mount Everest with her. "Not sure that fits into my schedule."

"Oh, come on. If you can get ice cream at Tucker's, you can go paint with me one night this month."

He refused to agree and Harper thought better than to push him. They barely knew each other. He wasn't going to give in so easily. She would try again when their relationship was a bit more established.

"Can I get a picture of you enjoying your lasagna? I was thinking since I'm here, I might as well tell people what makes Eagle Springs so special."

Wyatt's forkful of pasta hovered over the open take-out container. He had a jawline that Harper could sharpen knives on. She opened her phone's camera app and adjusted the settings. It was still too dark.

"Hang on." She got up and opened the curtains hanging over the window in his kitchen. Betty wasn't big and her windows didn't let in much light. Harper's followers would love the idea of her marrying a happy wanderer, who lived in a funky camper even when a perfectly normal house existed just down the lane.

She sat back down across from him. "Okay, that's better."

"How exactly did opening the curtains on a window the size of a postage stamp make that much of a difference?" he asked.

One side of Harper's mouth curved up. "Shush and smile."

Wyatt humored her and let her take a couple pictures of him while he finished eating. When he was finished, he threw away his garbage and led her back outside.

"You want some pictures by the hay bales?" he asked with his hands on his hips. Wyatt was dressed in well-worn blue jeans and a white shirt covered by a red-and-black-plaid button-down. He couldn't fit the part of cowboy better. His black cowboy hat shaded those hazel eyes.

Harper couldn't resist taking a few more pictures of him standing in front of Betty. "Can we do that or will your sister be mad?"

"She wouldn't be mad. She would have thought you were some strange woman trespassing if she had caught you out there alone. If I'm there, she'll just bug me later about why you were here and why we're spending time together."

"We'll be so fast, she won't have time to catch me being here." She pocketed her phone and started walking in the direction of the hay bales she'd seen on her way in.

Wyatt easily lengthened his stride to catch up with her. "Corliss has a list as long as I do to work on today. It's unlikely she and I will cross paths until dinnertime. In case she decides to check up on me, though, it's also really important that you don't tell her who your stepdad is."

Harper furrowed her brow. "What's the story with the Blackwells and Brock?"

"I don't want to put you in the middle of it. My gran and Brock have issues that go way back. It would be best to stay as far away from that as possible." It was a nice touch to make it sound like he was protecting her from the drama to get her to back off, but that wasn't going to happen.

"Don't you want me to find out from you? Otherwise, my only recourse will be to ask Brock."

"You can't bring Brock into this, Harper. You promised."

"I'm not going to tell him we're married, but I'm not afraid to tell him that I bumped into the famous rodeo star Levi Blackwell at the ice cream shop last night and wondered if Brock knew anything about him, which should lead to him telling me his side of this story."

It was Wyatt's turn to be confused. "How did you know my brother was a rodeo star?"

Harper held up her phone. "It may look like an ordinary phone that takes pictures, but it also connects to the all-knowing World Wide Web."

Wyatt frowned. "You googled Levi? Please don't tell me you have a crush."

"A crush on your brother? I'll have you know, I am a one-man woman, Mr. Blackwell. Did it ever cross your mind that I googled you and the newspaper writes more articles about Levi than it does a sweet cowboy-for-hire."

He actually seemed relieved. "Oh, right. That makes sense."

"You were a little jealous that I might have been interested in your brother," she teased.

Wyatt averted his gaze. "I don't get jealous."

Harper's grin widened. "You are a terrible liar."

"Is this where you want to take your pictures? I really need to get back to work. We have fencing that isn't going to repair itself all along the northern border. If we're going to do this, let's do it."

And just like that he had successfully avoided answering any of her questions. She knew that if she wanted him to cooperate with letting her stop by over the next four weeks, she would have to let that slide.

Harper carefully stood her phone up on its side atop one of the bales. The pasture was littered with a dozen giant rolls of hay. "So what are these bales doing out here?" she asked. "What's the point of having so much hay sitting in a field?"

"This is a grazing field. Horses and cows love to eat grass, but when winter comes around these parts, our fields are covered in snow. Every winter, we lay out a two-day supply of hay in each paddock. I'm sure that means little to you, but that's a lot of hay. I have to start making bales now so that when I'm done, this whole field will be smattered with them. Fall is the most important time for me to get bales made so that we have enough hay to keep all the grazing animals fed."

"*You* make these hay bales?"

Wyatt tipped up his hat. "I do. I have a big ol' tractor that helps me."

"The tractor rolls them up like this?"

"It does. It's pretty cool, actually. Maybe I'll show you the next time you stop by."

"That would be…fun." He was already looking forward to having her come back. For some strange reason that made her face feel warm. "I'm going to record a video of me cartwheeling in front of this row of bales, then I need you to pose for a picture in front of one with me."

"Sounds good."

Harper set up the camera to record once she was sure that the right spot would be captured in the frame. She had to remember this wasn't a real relationship. They were married, but she shouldn't get used to him wanting to spend time together. Harper needed to stay focused on her work. She pressed Record and then ran to get into position. She did three cartwheels in a row before jogging over to her phone to end the recording.

Wyatt started laughing. He was doubled over.

"What's so funny?"

"This is something your followers want to see? You doing gymnastics in a hay field?"

People always wanted to question the content, but she knew her followers like she knew herself. They would love it. And when they saw her standing next to her rugged cowboy husband, they'd never doubt she married for love. They'd all feel bad for her when she had to announce the divorce rather than laughing at her for getting married to a stranger only hours after meeting him in Vegas.

"Don't hate on my craft. I know it's not as exciting as making the hay bales, but it brings joy to people all over the world. That's what I sell better than anyone else—happiness."

"That's fair. You made me laugh today, which isn't always an easy thing to do. I guess if putting a smile on someone's face is your goal, I can't argue that you're not taking care of business."

She appreciated that he saw it her way. "Now, come over here. Stand right…here." Harper positioned Wyatt where she wanted him. "Stay just like this so that when I join the picture I can face in that direction," she directed. "My right side is my good side."

"Which side is my good side?"

He really didn't have a bad side, so it didn't matter which direction he faced. "Both of your sides are amazing. Don't worry—I'll make you look even better than you do all on your own."

Harper went back to her phone and set the timer. Before hitting the button to start the countdown, she made sure it was zoomed in and capturing the space she wanted it to.

"When I come over, we'll have a second or two to get ready. All I want you to do is stare at the camera and smirk. Would you mind if I gave you a kiss on the cheek?" she asked, not wanting to invade his personal space unexpectedly.

His expression turned. "Uh, no. I guess not."

"Okay, here we go." She clicked the button to get the timer started. She hurried over to him and wrapped her arms around his. She lifted one foot and planted a kiss on his cheek.

She could feel him tense as soon as her lips touched him. As quickly as it happened, it ended. Harper hoped that they'd only have to do that once. "Stay right there. Let me set it up again."

Harper checked the last photo and found it was amazing. The camera snapped the picture before Wyatt reacted to her kiss. Could it really be that uncomfortable for him? Of course it could. They weren't really together. He may have liked kissing her when they were in Vegas, but it didn't mean he wanted to do it again.

Harper wanted to do it again.

That was embarrassing to admit, even to herself. Kissing Wyatt led to nothing but trouble. Harper did not need any more trouble.

She set up the camera again and took three more pictures before she put Wyatt out of his misery. "That's it for today. Not too terrible, huh?"

Wyatt shifted his weight from one foot to the other and dipped his head. "I guess not."

"I'll let you get back to work. I'll call you tomorrow to see when we can get together again."

"Okay. This isn't going to be an everyday thing, though, is it?"

Apparently it wasn't not terrible either. "It's important for me to post every day, a couple times a day. Again, this is how I make a living. If I'm not posting and accumulating views, I'm not making money."

He adjusted his hat and sighed. "Do I need to be in the posts every day?"

"If you let me take some pictures in Betty, I could cut your time in half. I would be able to stage some pictures without you in them but make it look like we're together. What if I just came here when everyone was busy? I could be in and out and you'd never be the wiser."

Wyatt thought about it for a second as they started walking back to Harper's car. "I guess that would be okay. It's really important that you stay away from the main house. My brother is always working in the paddock in front of the large horse barn close to the house. That's where he's training some horses we just bought and where my sister, Corliss, tends to spend much of her time. Horses were our main source of income until recently."

"I'll steer clear of there. I'll only come by Betty, take some pics and leave." She was trying her best to be amenable, but she couldn't help but feel a little disappointed. As short as their time was together, she liked it. She enjoyed their banter and how he looked at her when she held her own.

"All right. Still call me before you come over in case something is going on and I think it's a bad time."

She gave him a thumbs-up. "Got it. I'll talk to you tomorrow."

"Hey, Harper," he called after her. She turned around to find him with his hat in his hands. He was so handsome it hurt. "Thanks for lunch. That was hands-down the best lasagna I've ever had. I'll have to check out Marie's sometime."

"Get the cannoli for dessert. It's one of the best I've ever had and I've been to a lot of restaurants all over the world."

He smiled and she realized how much she liked his dimples. "That's a ringing endorsement. I've never had a cannoli before, but I'll try it if you think it's that good."

"You've never had a cannoli? Now I'm kicking myself for not bringing you one."

He gave her a curious look. "You are very sweet, you know that?"

"Why do you say that like it's surprising?"

He chuckled. "I didn't mean for it to sound like that. Although, you do surprise me on the regular. You are not what I expected when I first saw you in that casino."

"I hope that's a good thing."

"Well, I married you, didn't I?"

They both laughed. "That you did, and see what you have to put up with now?"

"It could be worse," he said, setting his hat back on his head. "Have a good rest of your day, Harper."

Her heart beat a little faster. "You, too." She shouldn't be swooning, but she was.

CHAPTER SEVEN

WHY WAS IT that social media sites needed so much personal information to open an account? It was worse than applying for a credit card. He was surprised it didn't ask for his mother's maiden name and his social security number.

"All right, you need a profile picture," Mason said from his seat at Wyatt's small table. "Do you have a selfie on your tablet?" Wyatt gave him a look that answered his question for him. "So, no. Okay, well, we need to take a picture then."

Maybe this was a mistake. Never in a million years would Wyatt have believed he'd be asking his teenage nephew for help setting up a social media account so he could stalk his accidental wife who was busy posting fake honeymoon pictures all over the internet. His life was getting a little out of control. Wyatt liked things simple, uncomplicated. Having Harper in his life was anything but that.

"What if we skipped the picture?"

"You can literally put anything as your profile picture. If you want to put a photo of a horse, we could do that. Let me see what I can find on here that would work." Mason clicked through the apps on that tablet like some kind of savant. Wyatt used it to watch movies and play some games when he was bored. He had no idea how to do all the things this kid was doing right now.

"There you go. I found you a picture of a cowboy hat online. I saved your username and password so your tablet will automatically sign you in. You won't have to remember it every time." Mason handed the device back to Wyatt.

"That's helpful. Now what do I do?"

"What do you want to do?"

"If I know someone who has an account, how do I find them?"

Mason took the tablet back but held it so Wyatt could see what he was doing. "You click on this thing that looks like a magnifying glass. Then you type in the person's name you're looking for. Like if you were

looking for me, you'd put in *Mason Blackwell* and up pops people with that name.
Here I am, right here." He clicked on a tiny
circle with his picture in it.

"How did you learn to do all this? Is this
what they teach in school these days?"

Mason laughed. "I wish." He clicked on a
button that said Follow. He pulled his own
phone out of his pocket and started clicking
away. "You can't see my posts until I accept
your request to follow. Mom makes me keep
my account private, so I don't get catfished
or something."

"Catfished?"

"It's when somebody pretends to be someone else online. To be safe, I only let people
I know follow me."

"Smart. Is my account private?"

"I can make it private." He switched from
his phone back to the tablet. "Okay, I accepted your follow. Now you can see everything that I post. Promise me you won't
ever tell my mom about anything you see
on here."

Wyatt's eyebrows lifted. "What do you
post that you don't want your mom to know
about?"

"Nothing bad. Just things she'll want to know more about. She'll ask, 'Who's that? What's *her* name?' I never want to talk about girls with Mom. That is so embarrassing."

"I got you. Your mom will not learn about any potential girlfriends from me. My lips are sealed."

"Who do you want to follow on here? Is it that lady we met at Tucker's the other night? She was really pretty. Like, super pretty."

Even more embarrassing than talking about girls with your mom was talking about girls with your thirteen-year-old nephew. Wyatt snatched his tablet out of Mason's hands. "Thank you very much for your help, nephew. You can return to the main house. I will see you in the morning."

"I can help you find her. Do you know her last name? It's hard to find someone if you only know their first name."

Wyatt stood up and opened the door. "Good night, Mason."

"Wow, I can keep secrets too, you know."

"I don't have any secrets to share, buddy." Wyatt hoped he was a better liar than Harper thought he was. "Your mom is going to think we're up to something if you stay out here any longer. I don't want to answer twenty questions, do you?"

"True. I hate when she wants to play the question game. She never takes yes or no or 'I don't know' for an answer."

Corliss loved this kid like nothing else. She was a good mom. The best ones were always a little bit annoying because they cared. "Moms. They're tough. Thanks again for your help."

"You're welcome. Good night, Uncle Wyatt."

With Mason gone, Wyatt could focus on the biggest secret of his life. He hit the magnifying glass and typed in *Harper Hayes*. She was the first person to pop up. She had a little blue check by her name. No one else did. Did that mean something? He'd have to ask Mason tomorrow.

Wyatt clicked on her picture and her account popped up. Wyatt could see everything without hitting the follow button. Harper's account wasn't private. Didn't she know about these catfish? Then he remembered she had said she had millions of followers she didn't know. Did her mother not teach her about internet safety?

The first picture was the one she had

taken that afternoon by the hay bale. She had done something to the coloring; everything was much more vibrant than he remembered it being in real life. The sky was almost turquoise. She was kissing his cheek and the memory of how it felt to have her lips on his skin again made him feel like it was a hundred degrees in this trailer.

He'd had to use all of his willpower not to turn his head and kiss her right back. He might not remember marrying Harper in Vegas, but he sure remembered kissing her. It was unforgettable.

His thumb touched the screen where she made contact with his cheek. Suddenly, a heart popped up on the screen. "What did I do?" He tried to undo what he did by touching it again. This time the picture moved and another one appeared. He realized if he swiped left to right, he'd find more pictures from the day. There was one of him eating his lunch, one of him standing outside Betty and the video of her cartwheeling in front of the hay bales.

Wyatt's grin was so big it almost hurt. She was really good at this. She had captured these simple moments and made them beautiful. He didn't know how she did it, but she brought them all to life.

There was so much going on at the ranch. So many responsibilities. It was all falling on Wyatt to make sure things were taken care of while the rest of the family tried to make enough money to save the ranch. Gran was sick, but she would fight until her last breath to save the rancher home and the business she'd built from nothing. After all she had done for Wyatt and his family over the years, the least they could do was help her with that.

Even though he was busy beyond belief, there was always this niggling in the back of his mind. He would wonder what Harper was doing. He'd think about when he might see her again. He wanted to see her again.

Wyatt set the tablet aside. What was happening to him? He was so good at keeping his distance from people, at protecting his privacy. One night with Harper and he had let all his walls down, and she somehow kept convincing him to not put them back up.

There was a knock at the door. So much for enjoying a little solitude out here. Wyatt got up and pulled it open only to find his grandmother's brother on the other side.

"Thought I'd come say hello to my fellow RV enthusiast."

Wyatt wasn't sure he'd consider himself an enthusiast of anything, but he was certain he did not have a passion for RVs.

"Betty's more of a camper trailer, while you live in a motor home. Big difference."

"Potato, patato. Can I come in?" Big E climbed in before waiting for an answer.

Wyatt stepped out of his way. "Please do."

Big E took a seat at the table. "I've been trying to get to know everyone in my sister's family while I'm here. You're always the first one to sit down for dinner and the first one to take off. You never leave much time for socializing."

Wyatt stayed on his feet. Sitting down with the old man might encourage him to stay. "I have a lot to do every day so there's not much downtime."

"You're a hard worker. You remind me a lot of Delaney. She used to be the first one up in the morning and the last one to go to bed."

"She's been that way my whole life. Gran

never rests. Well, not until…" This kidney disease had forced her to slow down, to need help. Gran never liked to ask for help.

Big E nodded as he stared at his clasped hands on top of the table. "That's the thing about getting old, there's no running from it no matter how tough you are. I'm thankful we have time to reconnect. Losing touch with her has been one of my biggest regrets, and I have done plenty in my life that I should regret," he said with a wink.

"The fact that Gran hasn't called the sheriff to escort you off the property means she's not totally hating that you're here."

"I realize I only knew my sister for the first nineteen years of her life, but I assume she values family just as I do. I'd bet she's also stubborn and slow to forgive. Also like me. I'm hoping she'll come around. Let's talk about you, though. The Wanderer. That's what they call you. What's that about? Why the need to move around?"

No beating around the bush with this guy. Wyatt wasn't sure what Big E thought Wyatt was going to divulge here. Talking about himself was not his favorite thing to do.

"Nash is the only one who calls me The

Wanderer. He likes to make me feel guilty for doing what I want instead of what he thinks I need to be doing."

"And what is it that you want?"

"I enjoy traveling, seeing different parts of the country. It's also nice to learn how different people do the same job. Not only have I learned new things, I feel like I've been able to teach others a thing or two. That's really rewarding."

"I can see how that would be. Don't you miss being around your brothers and sisters? Working on the family spread?"

"I spent twenty years around my brothers and sisters, working the family spread. It was time to see what else was out there. Broaden my horizons, as they say."

Big E nodded, but he didn't seem quite convinced. His piercing stare seemed to be an attempt at reading Wyatt's mind. "Sounds like you're afraid of getting trapped anywhere with anyone for too long."

One side of Wyatt's mouth quirked up. "I've never felt trapped here."

"I didn't say you did. I just mean when you go from job to job, ranch to ranch, you are free."

"I do enjoy that perk of being a cowboy-for-hire. I work when I want, where I want. If I like it somewhere, I can extend my contract and if I hate it, I know I won't be there forever."

"My grandsons were all about broadening their horizons at one point, but they all came home and ended up staying."

Wyatt bit his tongue and chose not to inform his great-uncle that he was not like his grandsons. Wyatt was his own person.

"Your brother is struggling a bit to find his way in this new life. He sounds a bit like you—loved the travel when he was riding in the rodeo," Big E continued. "He's feeling a little lost."

"Levi?"

"Of course, Levi. If you start to feel a little bit like that, it's nice to know you've got someone who could relate."

Was Big E trying to get him to bond with his brother? He'd heard the old man was somewhat of a meddler. They weren't wrong. "Good to know."

"And your sisters sure understand what it's like to have a full plate. Corliss carries the weight of the world on her shoulders and that Adele is always burning the candle at both ends. She's got her hands full with the twins—that's for sure. I raised more than one set of twins in my lifetime, so I know how tough it can be."

"You really have been getting to know all of us."

"Nash has been the least forthcoming. He's excellent with those horses. I see why Delaney believes he can have them ready to sell by year's end. He is very single-minded. Suppose that's good, given the current situation."

"Nash has a talent that I certainly don't possess. Gran says he takes after our grandpa. Not sure if that's true or not since we never knew him."

"Your granddad did have a way with horses. It was like they spoke the same language. Cal Wesson was a true horse whisperer."

Gran didn't talk about their grandfather. Wyatt wasn't sure if it was because he had been gone so long she didn't think about him that much or if losing him so early in their life together made it too painful to talk about him. All he knew was Cal had died when she was pregnant with Wyatt's dad and his dad's twin brother.

"Did you know him very well?" It felt wrong to get information about his family from Big E. It was obvious that there was some bad blood between him and Gran. But Big E was the only person Wyatt knew other than Gran who had firsthand knowledge of his grandpa.

"We grew up together. Me, Delaney, Cal and your grandpa's brother Frank all went to school together. Cal was a wild one. Always in the thick of things. Trouble seemed to follow that guy around wherever he went. That was one reason it came as such a surprise when Delaney ran off with him. I didn't even know my sister liked him until then."

Wyatt tried to control his expression from giving away his complete surprise. He'd had no idea how his grandparents had met and gotten together. "That's why she was cut off from both families, huh?"

"She burned some bridges on her way out of town, and I'm embarrassed to say that I didn't attempt to mend them after what happened to Cal or at the very least after our parents passed. My sister has done amazing things on her own, but I wish I had been there for her, so it didn't need to be that hard."

"Gran raised her family to take care of each other, and that's what we do." That was his nice way of saying she didn't need Elias to come and rescue her.

Big E nodded. "She definitely did that. I know she hates that she has to ask you all to pitch in and that Corliss had to come to me for help, but I can't deny that I feel like this was a giant blessing. One that allowed me to reconnect with her and to bring our two families together so when she and I are long gone, you all know you've got family in Montana whenever you need them, and they can count on you."

Wyatt didn't know much about the Montana Blackwells other than what Corliss shared when she visited there. His sister had spoken highly of all of them. Wyatt's first cousins were in Texas and none of them were close since they left Eagle Springs.

"Well, you know who to call if you ever need a cowboy-for-hire up there."

Big E chuckled. "Oh, could you imagine what your gran would say if I stole you away?"

"She wouldn't see it that way." Gran might get a little jealous, but if Wyatt wanted to get to know his second cousins, she would be supportive.

"Maybe she'd give her blessing if I can help her figure all this trouble out. There's something bigger going on around here. I just know it."

Wyatt had no idea what that meant. It sounded pretty simple to him. The bank called in the loan and there were people chomping at the bit to get their hands on Blackwell land so they could develop it into something other than what it was. That wasn't going to happen if Wyatt and his siblings had anything to say about it.

"So, who was the lovely lady who came to visit you at lunch today? Old friend? An ex-girlfriend from your high school days?"

Wyatt was thrown by his sudden switch in topic and by the fact that he knew Harper had been there today. "When did you see someone come visit?"

"I was taking a walk to stretch my legs

and she drove past me. I waved. She waved. We had a little moment, I guess."

This was the reason it was a bad idea for Harper to come out to the ranch. It was a relief to know they hadn't spoken to one another. That could have been disastrous. "That was a friend. She came by to bring me lunch. No biggie."

"She doesn't work at the bank, does she?"

Now the reason for this line of questioning became clear. "She's not from here. She's visiting. You don't have to worry about her having anything to do with the trouble Gran is in."

"That's a relief. I'm suspicious of everyone these days. I keep telling your grandmother that there's a reason why someone is working so hard to take this place away from her, but she seems to think there's no reason anyone would have it out for her."

"Gran is a pillar of the community. I don't know who would have it out for her either. It's definitely not my friend."

"Good to know. She looked like a beautiful woman. Sometimes it's hard to stay friends with a beautiful woman. And women can get attached."

If Big E talked that way around Gran, it was no surprise she didn't let him stay in the house. In this Blackwell family, the women were equals. They didn't need to be handled differently or thought of as too emotional. Wyatt grew up with women who were leaders and didn't need a man to be successful.

His upbringing caused him to have so much respect for the strength of women. It was what attracted him to Harper. She was tough in her own way. He admired how smart and independent she was. Given how he couldn't stop thinking about her, it seemed more likely that he was getting attached than she was.

"You really don't have to worry about me. The two of us are very clear on what kind of relationship we have."

"You seem like a man with a good head on your shoulders. It's no wonder your grandmother speaks well of you. Does she know this friend of yours?"

Wyatt didn't want to be rude, but it was late and he wasn't interested in spending another minute talking about Harper. "Listen, I appreciate your interest in getting to know me better, but I have to get up early and my bed is calling my name."

Big E slid his large frame out of the seat and tipped his hat. "I didn't mean to overstay my welcome. One of these days, we'll have to find some time *before* the sun goes down to continue our little getting to know you chat."

"Sounds like a plan, sir. Have a good night." Wyatt opened the door and Big E saw himself out.

What a night. Wyatt grabbed his tablet and headed back to the bed. He scrolled through those pictures one more time. If Gran or Big E found out that he was accidentally married to Brock Bedford's stepdaughter, they'd come up with a million conspiracy theories.

Wyatt rolled over and unplugged his charging cell phone. He found Harper's number and hit the call button. She picked up almost right away.

"Wyatt?"

He'd thought he had a couple seconds to prepare, but she was on the other end of the line already. "Hey. Hi."

"I wouldn't peg you as a call-on-the-phone-to-chat kind of guy. Is everything okay?"

"Yeah, everything's fine. I'm just not so sure coming over here again is a good idea."

"Why? What happened?"

"I heard you saw my great uncle on your way off the ranch today, and that has led to more questions. I think we have to meet elsewhere when you need to get your pictures."

Harper didn't miss a beat. "I guess that means you're coming to Wine and Paint Tuesdays at the art studio in town."

"Oh, I… I don't know about that."

"Come on, it's in the evening. After dinner. It won't interfere with your work during the day." She sounded far too happy about this.

Wyatt ran a hand through his hair. He had to do something so she didn't come back to the ranch. "Tuesday Wine and Paint it is."

"Yes!" He could picture her raising a fist in the air. "I'll sign us up and meet you there."

"I'll see you there."

If it was possible to hear someone smile, Wyatt would bet this was what it sounded like. "I'm really looking forward to it."

Painting was not a skill Wyatt possessed.

He'd had to take an art class in high school and got a C. He had deserved an F, but the teacher had taken pity on him since his sister Adele had been her favorite student. Wyatt was not looking forward to the painting part, but spending some time with Harper didn't sound too bad.

"So am I."

CHAPTER EIGHT

HILLSHIRE ART LUCKILY HAD two open spots for Sip and Paint Night that Harper happily reserved. The woman who took her reservation was the same one who checked her in when she arrived Tuesday night. She wore a name tag that identified her as Jill.

"Harper Hayes. Yes, I see your name right here. You're the one who called to reserve a spot for Wyatt Blackwell, right?"

"He's meeting me here." She glanced back at the door. "Should be here any minute."

Jill pushed some of her hair behind her ear and averted her eyes. "I haven't seen Wyatt since high school."

"You went to high school with Wyatt?"

Her eyes lifted and that expression was a dead giveaway. Not only had she gone to high school with Wyatt, but she'd had a crush. A big one. "I did. We had some classes together. I don't know if he'd even remember me."

The door behind Harper opened and in walked Cowboy Wyatt. He wore a T-shirt that said something about a Cranky Crow and dark jeans. Instead of his usual cowboy hat, he was sporting a backward baseball cap. Harper felt the butterflies in her stomach all take off at the same time.

"I wasn't sure if we were meeting inside or outside. Oh, hey, Jill. How are you?"

Harper watched as poor Jill melted right in front of them. He had remembered her and she was over the moon and completely unable to form actual words with her mouth. "Iiii…ahhh. Hi," she managed to spit out.

Wyatt was completely oblivious to the effect he was having on her. "Bet you never thought you'd see me in a place like this, right? I have not used a paintbrush on anything but walls since I left high school. I hope we don't get graded on our work tonight."

Jill let out a nervous giggle. "We don't grade you. It's just for fun."

"I remember you were really good at art. It shouldn't surprise me to see you here. Has this place always been here?"

His compliment caused Jill's cheeks to flush bright red. "Yeah, Mrs. Owens owned it when we were in high school. I used to take classes here since I was little. She let me take over when she wanted to retire."

"Oh, wow. Cool."

Harper bit back a laugh. Wyatt had been sure this place was new. She tried to get Jill's attention. "Do you take credit cards?" she asked, taking out her wallet.

"I got it," Wyatt said, reaching into his back pocket for his wallet.

"You don't have to pay for me," Harper said. "We can go dutch."

"Let me treat since you brought me lunch the other day." Before she could protest, he added, "It's only fair."

She couldn't argue with that, and let him pay cash for their painting adventure. The fee included everything they needed to participate in the painting portion of the night and a bottle of wine to share.

"Are there assigned seats or do we just pick a spot?" Harper asked once Wyatt had paid. There were four long tables with three to four easels holding up canvases on each one.

Jill's eyes were still glued to him. "You guys can sit wherever you like. Everything you need is at your table."

"Thanks so much," Harper said. "Where do you want to sit, Wyatt?"

He picked a table away from the group of ladies who had already opened their bottle of wine and were talking loudly about the things their husbands were probably doing with the kids tonight.

"Oh my, you may have just made Jill's entire life tonight."

"What are you talking about?" he asked as he inspected the art supplies on the table.

Harper kept her voice low. "She didn't think you would even remember her. She clearly had a massive crush on you back then. The fact that you remembered she was good at art thrilled her down to her toes."

"Jill?" Wyatt's eyes darted between Jill and Harper.

"Oh, come on. You cannot be that obtuse."

He glanced back over at Jill, who had been staring at him. She immediately looked away. "Oh, wow. I think you might be right."

Harper covered her mouth to hold in her laughter. When she had herself under control, she dropped her hand. "You really had no clue?"

"She was pretty quiet in high school. We had a few classes together, but I don't think we talked that much. How could she know me well enough to like me?"

"Remember when I told you that those eyes of yours had probably broken some hearts? You stole Jill's with them. Trust me."

Wyatt rolled those sweet hazel eyes and went back to checking out the inventory. Harper decided to check out the wine selection.

"White or red?" she asked, holding up the two glasses.

"Whatever you like is fine."

Red it was. Harper opened the bottle and poured them each a glass. The cabernet sauvignon had a label she did not recognize, but it smelled amazing. She got out her phone and took a picture of the two glasses of wine with the bottle behind them.

The room was set up for ten people. It didn't take long for all the tables to fill up. Wyatt ended up being the only guy, and that made him very popular.

"You're one of Denny's grandsons?" one

of the women who took a seat in front of them asked.

"I am."

"How's your brother Levi doing? I heard his injuries were career-ending. So tragic."

"He's hanging in there. Recovering best he can. Don't you worry about him. My brother has big plans and will land on his feet in the end."

"I can't wait to see what he does next." She smiled and went back to chatting it up with her friend.

Harper set her wineglass down. "What kind of plans does Levi have?"

"I have no idea," Wyatt whispered. "I know he's been running ideas past Gran, Nash and Corliss, but I haven't been sticking around for those after-dinner conversations."

He made Harper smile. She could tell he didn't love socializing, but he always made an effort if someone tried to engage him. Just like that first night they'd met. He had been sitting at that blackjack table alone to play cards and pass some time. There had been no way for him to expect someone like Harper to take the seat next to him. He'd humored her every whim that night. Something told her it had most likely been her idea to get married.

"Okay, I think we're ready to begin," Jill announced.

Wyatt picked up a paintbrush. "You ready for this, Harper?" She nodded and he leaned close and whispered in her ear, "Promise me you won't post a picture of my painting if it's really bad."

Having his lips so close sent a shiver down her spine. His breath smelled like the wine and it made her want to kiss him so she could see if his lips tasted like it.

She swallowed hard and tried to play it cool. "I have a feeling Jill won't let you fail."

Ha ha, he mouthed as Jill began explaining what they would be painting tonight. She showed them what the finished product should look like. Jill unveiled a gorgeous painting of the mountains at sunset. They were painted in blues and purples. Below the mountains was a green valley dotted with pine trees.

"She thinks I'm going to be able to make that?" Wyatt said, leaning close again.

"All you can do is try. And if it doesn't

look good, have some more wine until it does."

Wyatt laughed and everyone turned to look at him. "Sorry," he mumbled.

Jill did a wonderful job of leading the group step-by-step so that they all managed to paint something that looked similar, yet inferior, to what she had made.

Harper took pictures during each part of the process. She even let Wyatt take some of her as she unsuccessfully tried to fix the crooked tree she painted in the valley.

"You are a much better photographer than you are painter," Wyatt mused aloud when they were finished.

"I'm going to take that as a compliment," she said with a laugh.

Jill made her way around the room to check on everyone's masterpiece. "How did we do over here?"

"Wyatt thinks I might need to come back for lessons."

"I did not say that. Yours is better than mine."

"Oh, sure. That's what you say now that Jill is listening." Harper poked him with her elbow. She held her phone out for Jill.

"Would you take a picture of us with our masterpieces?"

"Absolutely." Jill took a couple photos of them holding up their paintings. "I think you both did great," she said, handing back the phone. "But if one of you needs to come back for lessons, I think it's Wyatt."

Harper suddenly felt a bit more possessive than she thought she was. "Of course, you'd say that. You need to wait until next month, though, because he's mine until October."

Jill didn't know how to respond to that. Harper managed to make things even more awkward than they already were.

"Don't listen to anything she says," Wyatt interjected. "You did a great job tonight, Jill. I was worried that I wouldn't be able to do it, but you made it easy to follow along. We had a really fun time."

Her face lit up. "Thank you. I'm glad you had fun and I hope you'll come back."

"He wo—" Harper started.

"I'll try," Wyatt said over her. Once Jill moved on to check in with the other painters, he took the glass of wine out of her hand. "I think you may have had enough."

"Wait, no." She attempted to get it back. "I'm fine."

His expression clearly conveyed he didn't buy that for a second.

Harper tried to be a bit more self-aware. Her face felt warm and her muscles were loose. She was in that sweet spot between relaxed and tired.

"I can't drive home," she said before giggling uncontrollably. Oh man, she was tipsy.

"I'm not going to let you drive home. I'll take you and we can pick up your car in the morning."

"You were supposed to keep up with me, but you stopped after one glass."

"Well, the last time we both got drunk, *things* happened."

She was hit by those giggles again. "They sure did, didn't they?"

Wyatt glanced around as people started to stare. "I think we should grab our paintings and head home."

When they got outside, Harper realized she didn't want the evening to be over. She also didn't want to cause him more trouble tomorrow morning.

"What if we go back to Betty for a little

bit and once I have some coffee, maybe a nap, you can bring me back for my car. Then you won't have to interrupt your morning routine."

She couldn't help but notice his hesitation. He didn't want her to come to the ranch anymore. She liked the ranch. She liked him. None of that mattered, though, because they couldn't be together once they got an annulment.

"I could duck down in the passenger seat and no one would see me," she suggested.

Wyatt seemed to fight a smile. "Get in the truck. We'll go back to Betty for a little bit. I don't think I want you to return to Brock's house like this. You might start talking about me in front of him and get us in trouble."

"I just don't get it," she said inside the truck. "Why would it be so bad for people to know we're friends? Even if your grandma and Brock hate each other, would they really be mad that we get along?"

"Brock had my gran arrested right before I got to Eagle Springs, so yes, they would both be mad that we get along."

Harper shifted in her seat so she was facing him. "You grandma was arrested? For what?"

"I'm not sure I have the full story, but she went to the bank to talk to Brock and get some information and she may have accidentally hit someone or something. I'm not sure, but Brock called the cops or someone triggered the silent alarm. The only thing that matters is that she would be suspicious of why you would want to be my friend when there is bad blood between the two of them."

All the words he was using started to give Harper a headache. It was messy. That much was clear. They were never going to be able to tell his family who she was. It made her sad to think about never talking to him again once this was all over. If she came back to Eagle Springs it was possible Wyatt wouldn't even be here and if he was, she wouldn't be able to drop by his trailer to say hello. They would go back to being strangers.

"What's the matter?" he asked as they pulled onto the road leading to the ranch.

"Nothing," she said.

"Why are you crying?"

Harper touched her cheeks and sure enough they were wet. She hadn't realized she was getting herself worked up. How much wine did she have tonight? "Too much Cab Sav. I should have stuck to my limit of two glasses. One red, one white and I wouldn't have been blue." She was giggling again.

Wyatt shook his head. "Now I understand why you remember so little from that night in Vegas. You are a lightweight when it comes to alcohol."

"I'll have you know that I am a complete lightweight. That's why I usually just have a plain ginger ale and tell everyone it's got a little vodka in it."

Several windows in the main house were lit up. Different family members were probably settling in for the night in their own spaces. No one was outside, so no one saw Harper in the truck with Wyatt. Their secret was still safe.

Once they got inside Betty undetected, Wyatt seemed to relax. He got her a bottle of water out of his mini fridge. "Drink this," he said.

She uncapped it and took a long swig.

"I hope I didn't embarrass you in front of Jill. I think you two could be cute together if you decide to stick around Eagle Springs for a while."

"I don't think Jill and I have a future. She's very nice and an amazing artist, but once I do what I need to do here, I'll be back on the road, working where the spirit takes me."

Wyatt pulled a bag of pretzels from a cabinet and set it on the table. They both sat down. Harper was fixated on his shirt as she reached for some of the salty snack in between them. "What exactly is a Cranky Crow?"

"Ah, that's Harriet's place. Harriet is my gran's best friend. The Cranky Crow is where you go to get the best burger and brew in town or to play some pool."

"I see. Are we allowed to go there or is that off-limits since it's possible the owner might tell her best friend, a.k.a. your gran, that she saw us there together?"

"Good question. I will have to think about that. You should go there at least once while you're in town, though. With or without me, the Cranky Crow is a must-see when you're in Eagle Springs."

Harper played with the bottle cap from her water, spinning it on its edge until it fell flat. "What else is a must-see in Eagle Springs?"

"Hmm, you've been to Tucker's. Have you ever been to the hot springs on the outskirts of town?"

"You have hot springs around here?" Harper was a huge fan of hot springs. She'd once spent a whole week in Iceland at a geo-thermal spa thanks to her sponsors. "Can you take me?"

"I suppose so. We'll have to do that the day after I do some backbreaking work on the ranch. The hot springs are like magic on my sore muscles."

He had nice muscles. She started to reach across the table to touch his arm when she stopped herself. Touching him was a bad idea.

"I would love that. Hot springs have been shown to boost your blood circulation and improve your skin condition. It also helps you sleep better. I think it's sad that so many people in this country don't realize all the natural remedies the planet gives us. Too many women think they need to get plastic surgery or at least some stuff injected into their faces to stop the wrinkles from coming."

"Wrinkles are proof of a life well smiled," Wyatt said, grabbing a handful of pretzels for himself. "At least that's what my gran told me. She and Harriet are proud of their wrinkles."

"I love that. I try to be a body positive influencer online because too many people hate how they look instead of embracing what's beautiful about themselves. Take my mom for instance, she is gorgeous, but she constantly worries that if she gained five pounds, she would be completely undesirable to the opposite sex anymore. It's terrible the messages she gives herself."

"I think you and Gran would like each other."

Harper rubbed her palms on her thighs. "Too bad we can't ever get to know one another. Maybe after the annulment, we could just admit you know who I am."

"Let's see how it goes. I'm not totally against that idea."

That one concession made her feel a million times better. Maybe there was some hope for them yet. They spent the next hour talking about everything and anything. It was so easy with him. It didn't feel scary to share things with him and everything he opened up about just made her want to know even more about him because he was someone worth knowing.

"I should probably get you back to your car."

His offer dampened her mood. It was time to go, but all she wanted to do was stay. "Thank you for tonight. I know going to the painting party was out of your comfort zone, but I hope you really did have fun like you told Jill."

Wyatt's grin was mesmerizing. "I had fun, but I think it had more to do with who I spent the evening with more so than what we did."

Harper's heart pitter-pattered a little bit fast. She loved that he enjoyed being with her because the feeling was mutual.

"If you're not careful, Cowboy Wyatt, Jill isn't going to be the only one with a huge crush." She stood up only to feel immediately light-headed. The whole room started to spin.

"Whoa." Wyatt was quick to react and held her up, securely pulling her against him. "Are you okay?"

"I am now," she said, looking up at those hazel eyes. His kissable lips were right there for the taking. She couldn't resist, so she threw her arms around his neck and kissed him like she did back in Vegas.

He gripped her waist a little tighter for just a second before he pulled himself back. "That is going to get us both in trouble. I don't think we want to muddy the waters any more than they're already muddied."

Embarrassment heated her cheeks now. She ducked her head. "Sorry. I shouldn't have done that. I didn't mean to make you uncomfortable."

"Harper," he said, tipping her chin up with his fingers. "Nothing about that was uncomfortable. In fact, I would say you make me feel more comfortable than I've felt in a long time."

She'd take that compliment and try to forget about the kissing. Kissing would only lead to more confusion. Wyatt had been wise to stop it from going any further.

"We should go," she said.

Wyatt went to open the door when someone knocked on it. "Wyatt, open up!" someone called from the other side.

"Shoot," he said under his breath. "I'm going to have to ask you to hide."

CHAPTER NINE

W YATT'S GRANDMOTHER DID NOT take kindly
to being made to wait. She let herself in just
as Wyatt stuffed Harper in the bathroom.

"What are you doing?"

"I was in bed, Gran. What are you doing
out here so late?"

"You were in bed with your boots on?"

"I was getting ready for bed. I had just
been in the bunkhouse to use the bathroom
and was about to take off my boots and go
to bed. What's so important that you came
out here in the middle of the night?"

"What's up with the elk? I heard they
wreaked havoc on the fencing on the western side of the property. Is that true?"

"We had some damage. I told Corliss I
thought it was due to elk based on the tracks
I found."

Gran folded her arms across her chest.
"Your sister thinks that knowing things that

happen on my ranch shouldn't be shared with me because the stress isn't good for my health. What she fails to understand is that by refusing to tell me things, I get more stressed. From now on, whatever you tell your sister, you tell me. Are we clear?"

Wyatt held his hands up in surrender. "I was not aware she was editing what I told her when she talked to you. I will come to you directly with any new information about the ranch."

She dropped her arms back to her sides and exhaled slowly. "Thank you. I don't need to be treated differently because of my messed-up kidneys."

"I get it, but you should know that Corliss probably did what she did because she's worried about you. We all are."

"I'm old. Old people get sick and they die. It's the way the world works."

Wyatt knew that to be true, but hearing her say it out loud made his throat tighten up. Gran was a constant, like the sun and the moon. She was always there. Sometimes there was more distance between them than others, but Wyatt was comforted by the fact that if he needed her, he knew where to find her. When she died, things would never be the same.

He swallowed down that lump in his throat. "Doesn't mean we have to like it or help it happen faster than we'd prefer."

"Just don't treat me like I'm already gone. Okay?"

Wyatt reached for her hand and gave it a little squeeze. "Okay."

She smiled and then glanced over his shoulder. Her eyebrows pinched together. "Why do you have two of the same paintings?"

Wyatt turned around. His and Harper's paintings were propped up on the counter by the sink. He didn't know why she had brought hers in with her other than she was still a little tipsy when they got there.

"You don't like it?" He grabbed his. "I painted this. See, there's my signature." He pointed to the *W* Harper made him write in the corner.

"You painted that?"

"Did you know Jill Kiehn runs an art studio downtown?"

Gran was still staring at him like he had horns growing out of his head. "Of course I know that. I suggested it to Barbara Owens when she told me she wanted to retire. *You* took an art class at Jill's studio tonight?"

"I thought it would be relaxing."

"Why do you have two paintings, though?" Gran started snooping around. She took a peek into the bedroom area even though there was nowhere to hide in there.

"Jill gave me hers."

"Jill painted *that*?" She pointed at Harper's canvas. Clearly, Harper was not as talented as their instructor, but what else was he going to say? He couldn't tell her that he went out with Brock Bedford's stepdaughter and besides, the minute she met Harper, Gran would figure out where she fit in in Eagle Springs.

"That's why she had me take it. I don't think she felt like it was her best work."

Somehow Gran accepted that as a reasonable answer. "Remember what I said about keeping me updated. No keeping secrets from me, Wyatt. You know I always find out the truth eventually."

That was what scared him. He could only hope that once she learned about Harper, it would be after they were officially divorced. "I got it. Good night, Gran."

"See you in the morning," she said as she stepped outside. "And hey, don't lead Jill on. If you're going to start dating someone, don't pick someone who has been carrying a torch for you since high school. We both know that once we get the ranch paid off, it's unlikely you're going to stick around."

"I'm not dating anyone, Gran."

"Hmm, that's not what my brother tells me," she shouted over her shoulder as she began her walk back to the main house.

Big E's meddling was as irksome as Wyatt had been warned it could be. "Big E also thinks that you like being called Delaney!" he called after her.

Wyatt closed Betty's door just as Harper exited the bathroom. "I can't believe even your grandmother knew Jill had a crush on you in high school."

He rolled his eyes. "Don't start. Can we not talk about Jill anymore? We are in big trouble if Big E is telling Gran that I'm dating someone and specifically you. He saw you. He knows what you look like. If he sees you around town, he's going to do whatever it takes to figure out who you are."

"Well, he's going to think I'm someone named Jill when he and your Gran talk again. Maybe that's a good thing. They'll move on to more important things."

Temporarily, that might actually work. The problem with small towns was that even the tiniest things got gossiped about. No doubt the ladies at the wine-and-paint party would mention they saw him there with a blonde woman they didn't know. Someone else was going to note they saw Brock's new wife eating lunch with her daughter, who also happened to be blonde. The next thing they'd know, people would put two and two together and Gran would realize he was hanging out with Brock's stepdaughter.

Wyatt leaned against the kitchen counter and rubbed his temples in hopes he could stop the headache he could feel coming. "I'm not sure how we're going to keep this a secret much longer. Why do I think this is going to blow up in our faces?"

"It's not. It's going to be fine. You are worrying about nothing. By the time people start putting two and two together, I'll be long gone."

"Can't we sign the papers and start the annulment? You have some pictures. People would understand if you took a little break while on your honeymoon. Once you come back online, you can tell everyone I was a real jerk and you had to end things."

Harper stood in front of him and placed her hands on his shoulders. "Please hang in there with me. Let me meet your grandma. Tell her I'm here not because I am related to anyone but because I came here to escape the pressures of Los Angeles. She won't know Harper Hayes is related to Brock. Hayes wasn't even my mom's last name when she met Brock. No one will make the connection."

"You think I should let her meet you? You don't know my gran. The woman has a sixth sense. She'll know we're hiding something."

"She'll think we're lying about just being friends. Clearly, your uncle already thought that. I'm telling you, we can do this."

She was quite convincing when she wanted to be, but Wyatt was not ready to bring Harper out into the open. That could only speed up the whole truth coming out.

"I can't agree with that plan right now. I need to sleep on it."

"Fine. We'll sleep on it and talk about how we feel in the morning. Should we head out now? Is the coast clear?"

Wyatt wasn't sure it would ever be clear. The whole ranch seemed to have eyes. "We can't go yet. There's no way she's back at the house by now. She would see us drive by."

"Okay, then I guess I better make myself comfortable." Harper backed away and then jumped on his bed. She pulled out her phone.

"What are you doing?"

"Let's get some pictures of us hanging out in Betty. It will help us pass the time." She reached out a hand and used one finger to beckon him her way.

She had been tempting enough tonight. First, by being adorably silly and then, by kissing him. Now she wanted to snuggle in his bed and take photos. Of course, that was probably safer than the other things they could do to kill time in his bed.

He closed his eyes and said a prayer that

he would not make any more mistakes tonight. When he opened them, Harper was
patting the spot next to her on the bed.

They were fully clothed, they were not
going to kiss, they were only going to be acting for the camera. They'd kill a few minutes and then he'd take her home. He had
every intention of doing just that. Only after
they took some pictures, they started talking; five minutes turned into thirty, thirty
turned into an hour.

"When I was seven, I broke my right arm
and had to wear a cast for what felt like forever," Harper said, rolling over on her side
and tucking her hands under her cheek.

"When you're seven, two hours can feel
like forever."

"Right? It's so strange how time seems to
speed up the older you get. What I wouldn't
do to be able to slow time down. If I could
have a superpower, that would be it."

Wyatt mirrored her position on the bed.
"Oh yeah, what would your superhero name
be if you could control time?"

Harper pursed those pink lips of hers
while she took a moment to think. That

wasn't helpful in stopping him from thinking about kissing her.

"I'd have to be Captain Slo-Mo or something like that."

Wyatt snorted, he laughed so hard. "Captain Slo-Mo? That has to be the worst superhero name I have ever heard."

"Don't laugh at me," she said, giving him a shove. The grin on her face told him she wasn't really offended. "I am not good at things like superhero names."

He tried his best to control his snickering. "Obviously."

"What would you name me then?"

"Easy. You'd be called Timebender."

Harper looked impressed. "You are really good at naming superheroes. I think that's your superpower."

"That would be the lamest superpower in the world. No one would read that comic book or watch that movie."

Her giggles made him smile. Who was he kidding; everything about Harper made him smile.

Her expression turned pensive. "You know, when I broke my arm that summer, my mom felt bad for me so she bedazzled my cast with all these little crystals in every color of the rainbow. It was the prettiest cast anyone had ever seen. I forgot she did that."

"I can't tell if you and your mom get along or not. Sometimes when you talk about her, you seem like you don't see eye to eye."

"That's a good way to put it. I love my mom, but I don't always agree with all of her life choices. Brock is not my first step-dad. Or the second or the third."

Wyatt brushed some hair away from her face. "How old were you when your parents broke up?"

"They didn't break up." She bit down on her bottom lip. "My dad died when I was six."

He wanted to pull her close and take away any of the pain talking about that caused her. "I am so sorry for your loss."

"It was a long time ago. My memories of him have faded so much it's hard to know if they're real or just things I've heard my mom say over the years. I do remember that they were really happy together. I can picture them holding hands all the time and my mom used to smile at him like he was the best thing on earth. Sometimes I think that's why it's so hard for her to stick it out with anyone else. I doubt anyone holds a candle to my dad."

"I'm glad that what memories you do have are positive ones. It's a blessing to be able to remember the good times."

"I'm not going to lie—I also remember when he got sick. Losing my dad was the worst thing that's ever happened to me and my mom. That's why no matter what she does or who she marries, I am always going to be there for her because she's all I've got. She's my person. Do you have a person?"

Wyatt had to think about it for a second. He had a lot of people in his life, but the title of "his person" could only go to one of them. "I get along with all of my siblings, but I'm probably closest to my brother Levi. We are a lot alike. I'm not sure he's my person, though. Honestly, if you asked any of us, we'd all say Gran was our person. She's definitely the heart of this family. Even though we were raised by both of our parents, we were all way more afraid of disappointing Gran."

"She seems tough, but in a good way. I wouldn't mind having someone like her in my corner. Something tells me no one messes with your gran."

"No one but Brock."

She rolled on her back and pressed her palm against her forehead. "I forgot about that."

"Trust me, people might mess with her once, but they learn real quick not to do it again. Brock will unfortunately have to learn that the hard way." Wyatt didn't want to talk about Brock, though. Their conversation had stirred up some of his own memories. "There was this one time I tried to sneak out of the house to meet up with friends but ended up bumping into my sister Adele, who was also trying to sneak out at the same time. We literally collided in the hallway, which caused the dogs in the house to start barking. Barking dogs woke Gran and my parents. While Dad was busy yelling at me and Adele for attempting to sneak out, Gran went snooping farther down the hall and figured out Levi wasn't in his room. My brother had already snuck out earlier. Gran threw on a coat and went looking for him in her nightgown and boots. She caught him making out with his girlfriend at Lookout Pointe in our dad's truck."

Harper rolled back on her side, giggling. "He must have been so embarrassed."

"Oh, he was mortified. Funny thing is, both Adele and Levi blamed me for getting us all caught. Being the youngest means you're always the scapegoat."

"At least you have siblings. I feel like I missed out not having any."

Growing up in a full house was never boring. Wyatt loved his brothers and sisters, but being the youngest of five made him appreciate having his own space. He had enough people in his life. Until he met Harper, he felt no need to get close to anyone. Or so he thought. Meeting Harper had changed all that. He had never wanted to get to know another person as much as he wanted to get to know her. No one had ever been as interesting.

They spent the whole night talking about how different their childhoods were and how certain life events directed their journey so far. One minute, Wyatt was lost in her pretty green eyes and the next thing he knew, his alarm was going off.

They'd fallen asleep.

"I AM SO SORRY," Harper said for the hundredth time.

"It's not your fault, Harper. I fell asleep, too. It's going to be fine. I'm always the first one up anyways. No one could have seen us leave. I'll stop and get doughnuts from the bakery and say I was feeling like Mason needed to take the morning off from cooking for once."

"Mason cooks?"

"He's practically a culinary genius. Thirteen years old and he knows how to make homemade mac and cheese with those toasty little breadcrumbs sprinkled on top. He even knows how to make his own breadcrumbs. I can't even poach an egg."

"There are so many great videos on TikTok that can show you how to poach eggs and some tricks to do it even easier than the traditional way," Harper said, scrolling through her phone. "Here's one, right here. I'll text you the link."

Sometimes it was like she spoke a different language.

Harper's car was the only one parked on the street outside the art studio. He pulled up beside it.

"Well, we really need to work on learning to end our dates before we both fall asleep," she said. "At least we can remember last night. That's a bonus."

Wyatt nodded. He was happy about being able to remember last night as well. They had talked about everything and yet, he still wanted more. There was this strange feeling inside him, this desire to be with her as much as possible. "Not having a killer hangover is always a plus."

"You might be able to say that, but I may have overdone it last night."

"Maybe we'll get it right one of these days."

Harper's smile lit up her whole face. "You're still up for going to the hot springs with me?"

"Sundays I usually have a lighter workload. We could go once I finish my morning chores."

"I guess I'll see you then. Thanks again for driving me back to my car and for last night. I appreciate that you went painting with me, watched out for me when I got a little tipsy and let me take this." She held his painting on her lap. She had decided that they should swap, so they'd always have something to remember the other by.

"Thank you for the conversation and for not waking me up with any snoring or sleep-walking issues."

"Do you have a habit of sleeping with people who do that?" She eyed him curiously.

He scrubbed the stubble on his chin with the back of his hand. "I did when I used to sleep in bunkhouses instead of in Betty. That's one of the big reasons I got her in the first place."

"Ah, yes. I don't think I would want to sleep in a room full of cowboys either."

"But one is no big deal, huh?"

"Not just any one. Only a very specific one. I happen to be married to him," she said with a wink before getting out of the truck.

It was the first time it didn't raise his blood pressure to think about being married to her. If he had to accidentally marry someone, he could have done a lot worse than Harper.

She got into her car and gave him a little wave. As soon as he turned his attention back to the road in front of him, the giant RV that'd been parked outside the barn since he got to Eagle Springs drove past. Big E was becoming a problem that Wyatt couldn't shake.

CHAPTER TEN

"WHERE HAVE YOU BEEN? I was ready to call the sheriff," Brock said when Harper walked into the house.

She suddenly felt fifteen years old. "Sorry, I was hanging out with a friend and fell asleep."

"What friend? How did you make a friend when you've only been here a few days?"

"I am sorry that I didn't text Mom about staying out. That was inconsiderate, but I am twenty-eight years old and that means I am old enough to do what I want, when I want and don't have to answer to anyone." She set Wyatt's painting down on the kitchen counter. "No offense," she added, feeling bad for putting him in his place. She was a guest in his home.

Brock pressed his lips together and readjusted his tie. Finally, he said, "Your mother isn't awake yet, so she isn't aware that you didn't come home last night. Maybe it's better that way."

"I appreciate that you were worried about me."

He busied himself at the coffee maker and shrugged a shoulder. "Your mother would be devastated if anything happened to you."

Harper felt guilty. Her mother would have been beside herself if she had woken up to find Harper missing. She didn't know she was going to be spending the night. Her phone had died while she'd been at the Flying Spur because she hadn't charged it.

She couldn't believe she and Wyatt fell asleep. They were only talking while they waited for his grandmother to get back in the house. She should never have lain down because it didn't take much for her to get comfortable. Wyatt put her at such ease. He was funny and quite the storyteller. His life was so different from hers and she wanted to know everything there was to know about him. She could listen to him talk all day.

He didn't do all the talking, though. He asked questions *and* he listened to her answers. Wyatt was kind of the perfect guy. She was not going to have to work very hard to present him to her followers as the ideal mate.

"I'm really sorry for making you anxious this morning. I'm glad my mom is oblivious."

"Apology accepted. Would you like some coffee?" he offered. Brock wasn't such a bad guy. It made her wonder what happened between him and Wyatt's grandmother. What could she have done to make him call the cops on her? It would be too suspicious if she asked him. "Any chance I can convince you to come to a lunch meeting with me today? There's someone I would love to introduce you to."

"Sure, I don't have any plans other than binge-watching some TV with Mom."

"Mr. Howard is brilliant. He has amazing ideas for this town. I'd love to get you in front of him, so we can propose working together to bring his ideas to life."

"That sounds great. Whatever I can do to help, I'd love to."

"All I need you to do is explain to him what you do on social media. Pull up some of your accounts, show him your following, talk up your influence."

Harper froze. He wanted her to show this guy her social media accounts? Right now, they were full of posts showing off her new husband. The husband no one here knew she had.

She was in a pickle. Wyatt seemed so sure that telling the truth would cause so many problems, but if Brock needed her, maybe he would be willing to trade a favor for a favor. If she helped him land this deal with Mr. Howard, he would keep it quiet that she accidentally married Wyatt Blackwell.

The truth was, she hated not being able to talk to anyone about Wyatt. This way she could tell her mom about this amazing guy she met. Even if they were going to get their marriage annulled, this relationship wasn't nothing.

"I need to tell you something, but if I tell you, I need you to promise that it is going to stay between you and me and Mom."

Brock's forehead creased. "What's going on?"

"Promise."

He held his hand up like he was taking an oath. "Promise."

"I didn't come to Eagle Springs on a whim. I came for a specific reason. And that reason includes someone you know, a family that you know."

Brock rested his elbows on the counter and leaned in, his interest evident all over his face. "Go on."

"That family can't know why I'm here. If you want me to help you with this guy today, I need you to promise me that you will not do anything to change that."

"Okay, I'm intrigued."

"I need you to be more than intrigued. I need you to promise that you will not do anything or say anything to this family."

"What family?"

"The Blackwells."

Brock stood straight up. "What in the world are you doing getting messed up with the Blackwells? Harper, you cannot have anything to do with them, you hear me?"

That was the reaction Wyatt warned her about. "You don't have a problem with the whole family, do you? Just the grandmother, right?"

The crease between his eyes deepened. "How do you know that?"

"I met Wyatt Blackwell in Las Vegas right before I came here."

He stepped back and put a hand on his head. "Harper, you do not want to get involved with the Blackwells. Trust me. Wyatt's grandmother attacked me and others at the bank not too long ago. We had to call the sheriff and have her arrested. She's trouble."

"Wyatt and I accidentally got married in Vegas. I had to come here to talk to him about getting an annulment."

Brock's hand went from his head to his heart. "Please tell me you're kidding."

"It's fine. We can easily get it annulled. Wyatt is totally on the same page as me. There was just one little glitch."

"What was that?"

"I sort of livestreamed the wedding on my socials and everyone online thinks that I am currently happily married."

"You've been living here for almost a week and you haven't said a word about this to your mother?"

"It's kind of embarrassing to admit that you had a little bit too much to drink in Vegas and married some man you don't even know. That's why I had to pretend that the marriage wasn't an accident, so my followers didn't unfollow in droves. I'm telling you this because if you want to use my social media influence, then you need to help me keep my social media influence. That means you cannot tell Denny Blackwell that her grandson accidentally got married and plans to get an annulment at the end of the month. If you tell her, Wyatt will no longer cooperate with me so that I can save face online."

Brock removed his hand from his chest and rubbed his chin. He narrowed his eyes. "This is the wildest story I have ever heard. I'm an old man, Harper, and I have heard a lot of stories in my day, so that's saying something."

"Trust me, no one thinks this is wilder than me and Wyatt. He's been very patient with me considering he could have easily just filed the annulment papers himself."

"This could work for me," Brock said, taking a sip of his coffee. Harper wasn't exactly sure what he meant by that. "I will keep your secret, but you can't tell Wyatt that you told me either."

"I don't want to tell him that you know. He's not going to be happy that I told. He was very worried that because there's bad blood between you and his grandmother, you would out us."

Brock walked around to the other side of the counter and put an arm around Harper's shoulders. "Don't you worry one hair on that pretty little head of yours. I won't say a word to Denny Blackwell. We will keep her in the dark as long as you need her there. You and I are going to sit down with Mr. Howard today and we are going to make him a deal that he won't be able to resist. Then, we're going to transform Eagle Springs into the next Boz Angeles."

"Mom would actually love that. It would definitely make her feel more at home here."

"I'm glad you see it that way," he said, giving her a little squeeze. "You, my dear, are going to help me do great things."

Harper felt like this conversation went a million times better than Wyatt thought it would. Brock was a reasonable person. He wasn't someone hell-bent on ruining the Blackwells. Not that Wyatt and Harper being married should ruin anything for anyone. Everything was going to work out beautifully.

"MR. HOWARD, THANK YOU so much for meeting us."

Xavier Howard was a tall, slender man with sandy brown hair and a receding hairline. He was dressed to impress in a well-fitted gray suit and a crisp black shirt with a matching solid black tie. He wasn't from Wyoming any more than Harper was. The two men shook hands and they each took a seat at a table in the back of the Hightower Restaurant.

"You piqued my interest when you said you wanted to share with me a way to make money, Mr. Bedford. You know I love to do that."

Brock chuckled. "I do, I do. And the way we're going to do that is with the help of my very clever stepdaughter. Mr. Howard, this is Harper Hayes."

"It's a pleasure to meet you, Mr. Howard," Harper said, extending a hand.

He shook her hand and smiled. "Please call me Xavier."

"Xavier, Brock has told me you are the man who can help transform Eagle Springs into the perfect place for my mom to live. I couldn't not offer up my assistance in making that dream a reality."

Xavier sat back in his chair and crossed one leg over the other. "I'm interested in hearing more about how you think you can help."

"I am a social media influencer. Quite a popular one actually." Harper pulled out the tablet they had brought along to show off her media empire. All morning she worked on putting together a slideshow presentation basically selling herself as the perfect marketing tool. "As you can see here, I have millions of followers across multiple social media accounts. My last major post garnered 4.6 million views and over two million likes. I've already started showcasing the beauty that exists here in Eagle Springs, and I have no doubt that by working with you, we can make Eagle Springs, Wyoming, the next Aspen, Colorado."

Harper flipped through her presentation and continued her sales pitch. By the end of it, Xavier was grinning from ear to ear.

"Bedford, I may have seriously underestimated what you can bring to the table. Literally." He lifted his drink and Brock eagerly clinked his own glass against it.

"I'm glad we're on the same page. I can't wait to start working together," Brock said.

Harper truly appreciated Brock bringing her in on this opportunity. Not only did she now have the chance to make Eagle Springs more comfortable for her mom, being a part of this project meant that she had a good reason to stick around. Maybe she wouldn't have to be so quick to end things with Wyatt if they were going to be in the same place a little longer.

His grandmother might even end up liking her if Harper was able to put Eagle Springs on the map. His gran loved this town and Harper was beginning to feel the same way.

When lunch was done, Brock drove Harper back to the house. Brock owned a two-story log-cabin-style home on a decent amount of land. He had a horse stable but no horses at the moment. He had told Harper when she had been there for the wedding that he'd happily buy her mom a horse if she wanted one. Clearly, he hadn't known her very well back then. Horses weren't her mom's thing.

"I can't wait to see what Xavier has planned. This town has good bones. A little facelift, some new businesses to fill the empty storefronts, and this place could be perfect for people from the coast looking to get away," Harper said as they pulled into the driveway.

"Your mother would love a spa. They've got to be planning to put a resort in somewhere. There is some prime real estate around here that should be up for grabs soon enough."

"That sounds good. I think a luxury resort would be perfect. Not to mention a golf course. You guys really need a golf course around here. Mom would love that, too."

"I love the way your mind works. I think Xavier will be open to our ideas now that he knows we can bring the people to whatever we build."

It had been a long time since Harper felt this kind of purpose. She loved what she did, but most of the time she was only selling something that someone else made. This was a chance for her to have a say in what she was going to promote. She could take a special kind of pride in this venture.

"I'm actually looking forward to doing this with you. To be totally honest, I thought you were going to be like everyone else my mom has brought into my life over the years, but you seem to truly want my mom to be happy. You're also the first guy my mom has married that has seen the worth in what I do.

No one else has treated me like that. That what I do is meaningful."

"Well, I do love your mom and I want nothing more than for her to be happy. She gave up everything in Los Angeles to come here to be with me. I don't want her to regret it." He cleared his throat. "I wasn't lucky enough to have any kids of my own, so it means a lot to me that you are giving me a chance to be part of your life as well."

Were they...bonding? This was completely foreign to Harper. Even when she was little, her stepdads wanted very little to do with her. Could this be a chance for them to be a real family? She didn't want to get her hopes up yet, but this was promising.

Her mom was sprawled out on the enormous leather sectional couch when Harper went inside. Brock's house was very masculine. There was a deer head mounted above the fireplace. Harper couldn't believe her mom hadn't redesigned everything yet. She needed to get Serena out shopping as soon as possible. They needed to at least get some fall decor.

"How was your lunch?"

"It was kind of great," Harper replied, sitting next to her mom.

"Brock has been working so hard to get in on this deal with these people for a couple months now. I appreciate that you are willing to help him make this happen."

Harper rested her head on her mom's shoulder. "It might be kind of nice to get to spend some more time with you. If I work on this with Brock and Xavier, I can stay for a while. How would you feel about that?"

"How would you feel about it?"

"I feel good about it. I kind of like it here in Eagle Springs."

"You do?" She patted Harper's leg. "You and Wyoming small towns seem like opposites."

"Opposites attract sometimes, you know." More than her mom would ever know. Wyatt couldn't be more different from every guy she even thought about dating, yet he was one of her favorite people in the world.

"That wouldn't have something to do with whoever you went out with last night, would it?"

"I went to a painting party. Next time, you should come with me. There were a lot of nice ladies there that you might want to be friends with."

Serena sighed loudly. "You keep trying to get me to make friends. Do you think I've forgotten how to make friends? Do you think I need help making friends?"

"Have you made any friends since you moved here?"

Serena shrugged her shoulder to get Harper off her. "I don't need you to point out that I have not exactly been fitting in around here."

"Mom, I'm not trying to make you feel bad. I think that if Brock and I have our way, we're going to make Eagle Springs desirable to more people just like you. You'll have so many friends to choose from, you won't know what to do with yourself."

"So you're doing all this to make sure I'm not lonely?"

Harper roped her arm around her mom's. "I'm doing this because it makes me feel like I'm doing something special. It is also giving me more time with the people I love. Like you."

"And what about the person you bought that lasagna for the other day? You did buy that for someone else, didn't you? You're hiding something from me."

"Since I already told Brock, I guess I might as well tell you, too."

Serena shifted in her seat, so she was facing her daughter. "You told Brock before you told me?"

"Only because I had to, not because I didn't want to tell you first." Harper pulled out her phone and found one of the pictures of Wyatt looking extremely gorgeous. There were quite a few to choose from. "I met this handsome gentleman in Las Vegas." She handed her mom the phone.

"Oh my. He's…"

"Hot. I know. Turned out he was from Eagle Springs."

"The men of Eagle Springs do not look like this, Harper." She zoomed in on Wyatt's face and then pinched the picture back to normal. "None that I've seen at least."

"He doesn't live here anymore, but he grew up here. He's home visiting for a little bit. His grandma needs his help on their ranch."

Serena gave Harper her phone back. "You came to visit because you met this handsome man in Vegas and he told you he was coming here? He made that much of a first impression."

"I did find him to be very charming, but there's another reason I came to Wyoming. We sort of got married."

Serena's jaw dropped. "Harper Olivia Hayes. Please tell me that this is some kind of social media challenge prank."

"I know it sounds ridiculous. How does someone go to Vegas and turn into a massive cliché? Well, you win big in blackjack and then you celebrate with one too many bottles of champagne. That's how. We plan to get an annulment. It isn't going to be a real thing."

"Please tell me you were bringing him lasagna and annulment papers and he signed them right then and there."

Harper kicked off her shoes and pulled her knees up to her chest. "So, funny story. I may have live-streamed the whole experience and now my millions of followers think that I am happily married."

"Harper!"

"I know! I know what you're going to say. I promise you that we have every intention of annulling the marriage as soon as we can, but first we have to pretend that I didn't foolishly post the biggest mistake of my life all over the internet for the world to see."

"Honey, this isn't like you. You have always been so smart about everything you do. You don't get caught up in the romance of life like I do. I can't believe this happened."

"I'm starting to think that maybe it was fate. Maybe marrying Wyatt happened so I would come here and spend more time with you and help Brock get into this investment deal. I think that maybe all of this happened for a reason."

"What happens when this Wyatt sees that you're worth a whole lot of money and decides that he doesn't want to put an easy end to this marriage of yours? What if he tries—"

"Wyatt would never do that. He's not a material person. He lives in an old camper and owns about five things total. He is not going to take anything from me."

Serena shook her head. "I know you want to believe that, sweetheart, but you don't know anything about this man. Who knows what he's really like?"

"He's kind and funny. He holds the door open for me and stands up when I stand up. He listens to what I have to say and asks me about myself instead of just talking about himself. He's an uncle, the kind that takes his nieces and nephews out for ice cream. He's a really good man, Mom."

Serena's hand covered her mouth as her eyes went wide. "Oh no. It's worse than I thought. You're falling in love with him."

CHAPTER ELEVEN

WYATT WAITED ALL DAY for Big E to say something. He thought for sure he would do it first thing when Wyatt got back to the ranch with doughnuts. When he didn't show up for breakfast, he figured the old man would wait until dinner. The whole time they ate Mason's spaghetti and meatballs, Wyatt was prepared to answer questions about Harper.

But Big E said nothing. It was almost worse than being confronted. Wyatt started to wonder if he had already said something to Gran. She had been looking at Wyatt funny all through dinner. She even asked him to help clean up.

Wyatt rolled the sleeves of his flannel shirt up to his elbows. He started scraping the scraps of food left over into the garbage while the sink filled up with water. Gran busied herself with wiping down the kitchen table. Wyatt wasn't sure if he should engage her in small talk or not. She didn't say anything so neither did he. Gran moved to her spot next to him and silently dried the dishes he washed.

He'd never felt so guilty before even though it wasn't exactly like he did anything wrong. There wasn't anything truly bad about being friends with Harper.

"So," Gran said as they got close to being finished. "You gonna tell me what you told Corliss today?"

Wyatt exhaled the breath he had been holding since she'd started that sentence. Gran wasn't worried about Harper; she was too focused on everything that was happening on the ranch.

"I've been thinking it might be more cost-effective to put in some wildlife-friendly fencing that will keep the cattle in but allow the pronghorn, elk, and deer to migrate safely across our land. In the end, it will cost less to do that than replace broken fencing over and over again."

"What's that going to entail?" she inquired as she tossed the overly damp dishcloth aside and got a fresh one from the drawer in the island.

"I learned about wildlife-friendly fencing on one of my last jobs. It uses a lot less barbed wire. You build the fence a little shorter so adult animals can jump over it and you hang the bottom wire high enough for other animals to crawl under. That way we reduce tangling. You could also add gates, drop-downs or other passages in places where the wildlife tend to cross the most, like the spot I found the other day."

Gran picked up another plate and dried it carefully. "That's something you learned on one of your jobs, huh?"

"Guess my traveling finally came in handy for the family."

"Guess so." She picked up another plate. "Your brother and sister can help you with the new fencing when you're ready to get started on it."

Corliss had already offered her assistance and they were going to have Ryder help out on his day off. Corliss wanted Nash to focus on the horses. Gran still needed to feel like she was in charge though, so Wyatt just nodded.

Big E returned to the kitchen. "Nash has

something to show you, Delaney. Why don't you let me take over?"

"Figures you'd offer to help when we were practically finished," she grumbled, tossing him the dish towel.

Wyatt kept his eyes focused on the dish in his hands as Big E took the spot next to him. This was it. This was when he was going to confront him. Wyatt decided to beat him to the punch.

"Didn't realize you were such an early riser."

"I've been rising before the sun since you were in diapers, son."

"I'm sure you have." Wyatt waited for him to ask him about Harper, but Big E dried the dishes placed on the drying rack without saying a word.

Wyatt shifted uncomfortably. Thankfully, he scrubbed the last of the silverware clean. "Always thought Gran should have installed a dishwasher in this place, but anytime one of us grandkids would mention it, she'd always say, 'Why would I spend money on an appliance when I have five perfectly good dishwashers right here.' It's always been the chore we all dreaded. You always knew you were in trouble if Gran put you on dish duty."

"My sister is a tad more practical than I am. I have never met a dishwasher I didn't like, and making your grandkids load and unload is still decent punishment when they misbehave. What did you do to deserve dish duty tonight?"

Wyatt let out a nervous chuckle. "Oh, that was when we were kids. Now that we're all adults, if we're in trouble, Gran just cusses us out. She doesn't have to be subtle about it anymore."

Big E nodded and set the dish towel down. His expression turned wistful. "Maybe we are more alike after all."

"I can put the dried dishes away. If you want to go join everyone else, I'll finish up," Wyatt offered, hoping his great-uncle would move along and end his torture.

"You aren't much for hanging out with the family after dinner, are you? You must have things to do, people to see."

"The only thing I do after dinner is get ready for bed."

"Your gran might believe that, but us early risers know different, don't we?" And out the door he went, leaving Wyatt cursing himself. If he was going to convince Big E and his gran that he wasn't up to anything that they should be concerned about, he would have to stay and hang out with the family.

"Hey, Uncle Wyatt, where do you think is the best fly fishing? Yellowstone National Park or in Jackson Hole?" Mason asked when Wyatt joined everyone in the family room.

Wyatt took a seat on the floor and stretched his legs out in front of him. "Right now is a great time to go to Jackson Hole and fish the Snake River. They also have Flat Creek, which is the first fly-fishing-only stream in Wyoming."

Nash shook his head. "Oh, come on. Yellowstone has more lakes and streams than anywhere else in Wyoming, and the trout is the absolute best there."

"You're not wrong about that. Yellowstone has some great fly-fishing, too," Wyatt said. "But if you want to go somewhere really cool with excellent fly-fishing, I would send you to Flaming Gorge Reservoir down by the border of Wyoming and Utah."

"Oh, I've been there before," Ryder said, joining the debate. "That is a gorgeous area, but you have to go in early spring for the best trout and salmon out there."

"Late summer they have some pretty active bass. It just depends on what you want to catch," Wyatt added. "Last summer, when I was working at this ranch in Utah, me and some guys did a weekend at Red Canyon Campground and fished in the Green River down there."

"You've been to so many cool places," Mason said. He tossed a pillow at his mom. "Why don't we go to cool places like that?"

Corliss picked up the pillow and bopped him over the head with it. "Eagle Springs is the coolest place in the world. Why would you need to go anywhere else?"

Everyone, even Gran, snickered at that.

Mason rolled his eyes. "You are so lame, Mom."

That earned Mason another smack with the pillow. Nash disarmed Corliss and shoved the pillow behind his back. "If we get the ranch on its feet again, maybe you all can take a family vacation next spring and decide for yourselves which place is the best."

"When, not if," Corliss corrected him. "And *when* we get the ranch on its feet again, I will be needed here to keep it that way."

"The ranch will survive a week without you, Corliss," Gran said, chiming in. "I wish someone would have reminded me of that when I was your age."

Corliss and Nash exchanged a look. "Then you'll have to come with us on this family vacation," Corliss suggested.

Gran seemed smaller tonight as she sat in her chair, the oversize forest green tufted wingback that she always retreated to after dinner. She glanced at each one of her grandkids before staring down at her hands. "We'll see."

The whole room fell silent as the weight of their grandmother's illness hung heavy in the air. Would Gran be alive this time next year? She wasn't going to live forever, that was something they all knew to be true, but the end had never seemed so near. Wyatt swallowed down the growing lump in his throat.

"I can always come back to help out around

here when you go on this big vacation," he said, trying to shift the conversation back to safer territory. "You could leave knowing the Flying Spur was in good hands."

"Already trying to think of a reason to come back to Eagle Springs, are ya?" Big E said. "Maybe you're finding more reasons to stay than leave again."

"Artsy reasons," Gran muttered with a sly smile. She and Big E shared a little chuckle.

"Artsy reasons?" Nash's scrunched-up face meant he had no idea what they were talking about. At least they hadn't been gossiping with the rest of the family yet.

Wyatt realized the elder Blackwells both thought they were so smart. They believed Wyatt and Jill were an item. Gran had seen the painting that Wyatt claimed was Jill's and Big E saw him drop someone off right outside the art studio. Harper was right. They both jumped to the conclusion that she was Jill because Big E was the only one who had actually seen her.

Wyatt's whole body relaxed. They were safe for now. "I would definitely come back to help out if it means Mason gets to go fishing where the trout are the size of Olivia."

"What?" Olivia giggled. "There are fish as big as me?"

"Don't you weigh about twenty pounds?"

"No way. I'm not twenty pounds. Right, Dad?"

"You haven't been twenty pounds since you were about one years old," Ryder said. "I think your uncle is teasing you."

"Or has no idea how much babies weigh," Corliss said.

"I know how much a baby weighs," Nash said as if that made him somehow smarter than Wyatt. "I even know how much baby horses weigh."

"I was teasing her like Ryder said," Wyatt clarified, feeling like this was a good time to retire back to Betty. "I don't know about you guys, but I am exhausted. I think I'm going to turn in."

"Come on, we were giving you a hard time. Don't leave now," Nash said as Wyatt got to his feet.

"I'm not going to bed mad. Don't worry. I really am tired."

"Stayed up too late last night and got up too early this morning," Big E said.

"That must be it," Gran said with a nod and a smirk.

These two and their inside jokes were almost too much. "Good night, everyone."

BACK IN BETTY, Wyatt got ready for bed and slipped under the covers with his tablet in hand. He decided to check in on Harper's social media. Today, she had posted the pictures from the art studio and one of them lying next to each other in his bed.

The pictures reminded him of what a good time they'd had together. It was so easy to have fun with Harper. She found ways to bring joy to any situation.

As if she knew he was spying on her account, his phone rang and the caller ID told him it was Harper.

"Hey there, I was just thinking about you," he admitted.

"That must be why I felt like I should call."

"How was your day?" he asked, genuinely wanting to know.

"I had a really amazing day, actually. How about you? Did you get all of the things on your sister's list done?"

"I sure tried. Corliss sometimes forgets I

am only one man. Today, she wanted me to fix the air-conditioning in her ancient car. I'm a jack of many trades, but I am not a miracle worker. I did my best, but that thing is still on its last leg."

"It was nice of you to try, at least. I was able to spend quality time with my mom and my stepdad today. I even think I found a reason to stick around Eagle Springs a little longer."

Wyatt noticed the way his heart leaped at those words. Having Harper around seemed too good to be true, though. "Longer? Why?"

"Would it be bad if I was in town longer than the end of the month?" Her voice gave away her fear.

"No, it would not be bad. I didn't mean for it to sound like it was bad. Who do I have to thank for helping you stay longer?"

He heard her laugh lightly. "I can't tell you much because I'm not at liberty to talk about it yet, but let's just say that I might have found a use for my skills that'll help Eagle Springs."

"Help Eagle Springs do what?"

"Be all it can be," she answered without explaining.

"Truth time—I had my nephew create a social media account for me so I could see what you're posting about me. Us," he added. "You are very good at taking ordinary things, like me, shining them up and making them pretty. Eagle Springs is in good hands."

"First, I can't believe you made an account. Second, you, Cowboy Wyatt, are anything but ordinary. Have you read the comments on my posts? People love you. There are going to be ladies out there who will be overjoyed when we announce our divorce because it will mean you are back on the market."

"I don't know about that. I think your followers like your stuff because they like you. They'll forget all about me when we end things." Wyatt didn't want to end things. He couldn't say that, though, because he had made a deal. Pretend to be happily married. He wasn't supposed to actually be happily married. This marriage had a shelf life.

"Would it freak you out if I told you that

I get sad when I think about us ending things?" she admitted.

Hearing her say out loud the things he was trying to hide was such a relief. "It doesn't freak me out as much as the fact that I feel the same way."

"Yeah?"

"But the smart thing to do is stick to the plan, right? It's nice that we're getting along, but it's weird to think we could make this into something more," he said, hoping she'd disagree. He wanted her to say that anything was possible and they should wait and see how things go.

"Right. The plan is smart. We should definitely stick to the plan."

Wyatt's hope came crashing down in a ball of fire and smoke. Harper felt sad about their impending breakup but not enough to veer from their plan. It was silly to think they could be more than whatever this was. This was friendship, at least the beginning of a friendship, and he would consider Harper a friend after all this was over because having nothing to do with one another was no longer an option in his opinion.

"I'm glad we're on the same page. It will make everything easier in the end."

She got quiet for a second. "Exactly."

Wyatt had to accept his fate. "Oh, I have some good news. My grandmother definitely thinks that I am dating Jill from the art studio. My great-uncle also thinks that you are Jill. We have that tiny safety net until Big E stumbles upon the real Jill and realizes she is not you."

"Okaaaay," she said, stretching out the sound in the middle. "Would it be so bad if they knew I wasn't Jill? I mean, what would happen if our families knew we were friends? Your brother, nieces and nephew already met me. If we want to be friends when all this is over, wouldn't it be best if everyone knew we were currently part of one another's lives?"

As much as Wyatt wanted everything to be out in the open, Gran was not in a good enough headspace at the moment to handle Brock's stepdaughter being his friend. The loan being called in had soured her too much to be welcoming to anyone even remotely related to the bank manager.

"We agreed the plan was solid and that

plan includes that no one in our families can know that we're married. My gran and your parents can't know that we even know each other. It's the only way this can work."

"I get that, but I hate secrets and somehow, I have gotten myself into a situation where I am keeping secrets from just about everyone."

Wyatt could sympathize. He wasn't the kind of person to keep secrets either. He valued honesty. "I know how you feel."

"I want you to know that I am usually very straightforward. I don't want you to think I'm some sort of duplicitous person."

Throughout this whole ordeal, Wyatt had never gotten the impression that Harper was a bad person. "Each one of us has asked the other to keep secrets. If I hold that against you, then I have to say the same about myself."

"How do you do that?"

"What?"

"Say the right things all the time."

"Ha. I don't know about that." Lately, it seemed like whatever Wyatt said sent him deeper into the hole he was digging for himself. The fact that he got out of family dinner tonight without raising more suspicion was a miracle.

"Can I see you before Sunday? I'd really like to," Harper said, causing Wyatt's heart to flutter. She was turning him into some kind of romantic sap.

"Maybe. What did you have in mind?"

"I read that on Friday night, Neptune is going to get the closest to Earth as it can and be fully illuminated by the sun. This astronomy group is meeting somewhere called Eagle Ridge to look at it through this telescope."

"You found an astronomy group that's going to be looking at Neptune this Friday?"

"You keep forgetting that my job is about hunting down experiences in places that people don't know about. Come on, it's a once in a lifetime experience. Who knows when Neptune will be on full display like this again."

How could he say no to that?

CHAPTER TWELVE

THE WORST THING about having plans was that if you were looking forward to going out, time seemed to slow down exponentially. Harper had done her best to distract herself by taking Serena shopping to decorate the house for fall. They had gone with a white, black and gray theme. They found pumpkins and lots of buffalo plaid. Her mom seemed excited to get home and put everything out.

Of course, when Harper started getting ready for her fake date with her accidental husband, time started moving too quickly. Clothes were scattered all over her room. She was in the process of trying on outfit number six. She wanted to be casual but cute. It shouldn't look like she was trying too hard but didn't want to appear as if she hadn't put some thought into it. Time was running out. Wyatt was going to be there any minute.

"What happened in here?" her mother asked from the doorway.

"Does this look okay? If I curl my hair, will it seem like the right balance between casual and classy?" She had on jeans and a pale blue sweater. Her plan was to wear brown boots and minimal gold jewelry.

Her mom reached down and picked up the white T-shirt that had been discarded early in the process and the plaid button-down that was more like a light jacket than a shirt that she originally tried on with her black cropped tank top. "I like these with those white boots with the thick black soles. Layered necklaces, hair down with a little loose curl would be—" She gave a chef's kiss.

Harper looked it over. Her mother was completely right. "Thank you," she said with a relieved sigh. She should have gotten Serena's opinion earlier and saved herself from all this anxiety.

"What are you getting ready for exactly?"

"I'm going to meet up with the Eagle Springs Astronomy Club to look at Neptune in opposition."

"Who is Neptune in opposition with exactly?"

"I guess that means it's opposite the sun? I have no idea. I just know that we're supposed to be able to see it tonight."

Serena sat on the bed and folded her arms. "*We* being?"

"Wyatt and I are going together. I need new pictures to post."

"Right," Serena said with thick skepticism. "You need new pictures. That's what's driving this date night."

Harper stripped off the blue sweater and pulled on the white T-shirt. "Don't start. We are doing these things to keep up online appearances. He has been very honest about wanting to stick to the plan of parting ways at the end of the month."

"Does he know that you've been having feelings?"

Being completely truthful with Wyatt had been too scary. She admitted that she wasn't looking forward to the end and he admitted he wasn't either. As quickly as he told her he was feeling similar to her, he yanked the rug out from under her by professing his faith in their plan. Their plan to break up and walk away.

"We have both agreed that it's best to stick

to pretending we have decided to go our opposite ways at the end of the month."

"But things have changed. You could be out here much longer now that you're going to be working with Brock. If you're here and he's here, you won't be going in different directions. You'll be sharing the same space."

Harper had decided it was easiest to remain in the mindset that this was temporary. That way if things went as they planned, she wouldn't feel hurt. If she got her hopes up and things didn't work out, she'd be crushed. And if by some odd chance, they stuck to the plan but then found that they belonged together in the end, she could simply enjoy the unexpected outcome.

"I'm not going to put any expectations on what's going on. Wyatt and I get along, which is super helpful. You know me—I am not one for making a long-term commitment. Even if I do help Brock with things around here, eventually, I would have to get back to my normal life."

"You're going to have to settle down someday, Harper. You can't live alone on the road forever."

Taking advice from Serena on anything

other than fashion had always been a big no-no. "Mom, I am not alone. I have my friends. I have my followers."

"Your followers are not actual people in your life. They don't know you. They aren't there for you. You are a source of their entertainment. You need real people around you. You deserve to have love. To give it and to receive it."

"Why? So I can end up getting hurt in the long run? So I can have a string of divorces to add to my list? I've seen how the world works. I know way more people who get divorced than who live happily-ever-after. Heck, I know more people who have broken up during their engagement than have actually made it to the altar."

Serena reached for Harper and pulled her down on the bed next to her. "I know I have not been the best role model when it comes to how to have a successful marriage, but that doesn't mean that you couldn't choose more carefully than I did."

"You chose carefully with Dad and look how that turned out."

Her mom's head dropped. Serena gave Harper's hand a squeeze. "You can't be afraid to love because you think something tragic could take it all away. Your dad never would have wanted you to shut your heart down because of what happened to him."

It wasn't what happened to him that caused Harper to shut her heart down; it was what happened to her mom after what happened to him. Harper had watched her mom completely fall apart and struggle the rest of her life to hold it together. Love wasn't worth it. The amount of pain that came with loss simply couldn't be worth it.

"Don't worry about me, Mom. I have everything I could want. I'm happy."

Serena reached up and cupped Harper's cheek. "Believe it or not, I will always worry about you, sweetheart. I know that I make it hard for you to believe that sometimes, but you are the most important thing in my life."

Harper leaned into her touch. "I know, Mom."

"Go finish your hair so your husband will kick himself every day of his life for letting you get away."

Harper let out a breathy laugh. Her mom gave her another squeeze and left her to it.

In no time, Harper finished getting ready.

Her phone rang as soon as she unplugged her curling iron. Wyatt was there and waiting outside the house.

"You sure you don't want to come in and say hello to the in-laws?"

Wyatt's reply was lightning fast. "I'm positive."

Harper smiled as she grabbed her things and ran out to meet him.

"WYATT BLACKWELL?" A man with a University of Wyoming sweatshirt gawked at Wyatt and Harper as they approached the group.

"Do you know everyone?" Harper whispered.

"Small towns. I warned you," he whispered back with a blanket tucked under his arm. "Mr. Littlejohn, how are you?"

"I didn't know you were back in town."

"Just got back. Been here about a week. Since when do you run the Eagle Springs Astronomy Club?"

"My wife and I decided to organize a club about two years ago, and it was quite a surprise when it took off. We have twelve members. It's pretty awesome. Are you planning to join full-time or just wanted to see Neptune tonight?"

"Ah, honestly, I'm here with my friend. This is Harper. Harper, this is Mr. Littlejohn—he was my Earth Science teacher in high school."

Harper shook hands with Mr. Littlejohn. He was about her height and had wireframed glasses and a balding head. "I saw your writeup in the paper about this viewing and I was so intrigued that I begged Wyatt to come with me. I'm from LA, so the only stars I see are the ones who live in the Hollywood Hills. The sky is a big ol' mystery to me."

Mr. Littlejohn's eyes lit up. "You are in for a real treat then! Here in Wyoming, we have some of the least light-polluted skies in all of the United States. If you want to see the stars in the sky, this is the place to be."

"I don't think I've ever been able to see any other planets before. Tonight is going to be a first."

"I like your friend, Wyatt. She has the right kind of enthusiasm." Mr. Littlejohn leaned in closer to Harper. "Earth Science wasn't his favorite subject in school. I tried telling him that my class would help him be a better rancher, but he didn't believe me."

"We studied hurricanes for a whole month. You want to know how many hurricanes we've had to prepare for on the ranch?" Wyatt said in his defense.

Mr. Littlejohn didn't back down. "We also spent quite a bit of time on natural resources and conservation. We learned that ranches have just as many different plants and animals as some protected wildlife refuges. Ranches and earth scientists can do a lot of good for this planet working hand in hand."

"I love that," Harper said. "I'm very interested in climate control. I think that we need to protect this planet for future generations."

"I like you," Mr. Littlejohn said. "I like her, Wyatt. Welcome to our club."

Mr. Littlejohn left to greet some other stargazers, so the two of them went to find the best viewing spot. Wyatt spread the blanket out on the ground and Harper sat down and lay back.

"I couldn't imagine living somewhere everyone knows everyone. I grew up all over the place and I never was there long enough to get to know more than a handful of people, and none of them probably remembered me after I left."

Wyatt joined her on the blanket. He took off his hat so he could lie flat. Their arms were touching ever so slightly. He smelled good. He wasn't the kind of guy to wear cologne. He simply smelled clean, like soap. She wanted to rest her head on his chest and breathe him in.

"Well, around here, the only place I felt like I could put my guard down was out in the pastures on my horse with the cattle. The cattle might have known who I was but they never told Gran if they saw me do something I shouldn't or reminded me of embarrassing things I did when I was five."

"It's like you had to constantly be who people expected you to be because they knew what to expect."

Wyatt sighed. "Yeah, something like that."

"I don't know which is worse. Living up to an expectation or having the opportunity to constantly redefine yourself. Sometimes I think I forgot who I was because I was trying so hard to be who people wanted me to be. But the people kept changing and so did what they wanted."

"How come when you got the chance to settle down somewhere, you didn't take it? You chose a profession that sends you all over the place and you spend all your time trying to be something to a bunch of people online."

Harper pushed up on her elbows. "Woah, did you just psychoanalyze me?"

"I'm not judging you. I'm truly curious because I felt like I had all these people wanting things from me growing up, so the first chance I got, I hit the road. I couldn't wait to go somewhere no one knew who I was."

Harper lay back down and stared up at the vast Wyoming sky. It was a valid question. She had never learned how to put down roots. Staying in one place became too scary. What if she got attached and then things, people got taken away?

"Honestly, I think I've been too afraid. What if I chose to settle down and I didn't fit in?"

"Are you kidding me?" Wyatt rolled to his side. "You fit in everywhere you go. You've barely been here a week and every time we're together, you fit in better than I do."

"I'm good at first impressions, Wyatt. That's what I've been trained to do. But what happens when I stay longer than a week? What if I wear out that welcome?"

He reached over and cupped her face with his hand. His thumb gently brushed her cheek. "You don't give yourself enough credit. I think there are people who have met you and missed you a whole lot when you left. I know I will."

Harper's heart was beating so hard she couldn't believe he didn't hear it knocking against her ribs. Wyatt's eyes were locked on hers. She couldn't break free if she tried. Her mouth went dry and she had never wanted someone to kiss her as much as she wanted Wyatt to lean down and plant one on her lips.

"You say that now, but we'll see if you feel the same way at the end of the month."

"Trust me, you're talking to the guy who tries very hard not to get attached and you, my dear, are making it very difficult not to fall hard."

He moved a little closer, so close their lips were almost touching. Harper closed her eyes when Mr. Littlejohn called out for everyone's attention, causing Wyatt to pull away. Harper tried to get control of her breathing. It was a good thing she was lying down because she definitely would have fainted.

"Thank you all for coming out tonight. We have set up our telescope because even though Neptune is going to be the brightest it's been all year, it's still very hard to see without some help. For those of you who are new to astronomy, Neptune is right between the constellations Pisces and Aquarius. Everyone will get a turn to look at it through the telescope. While you wait your turn, simply enjoy the view."

"Do you want to go look at Neptune?" Wyatt asked.

Harper was still working on regulating her breathing. What she really wanted to do was be alone with Wyatt so he could finish what he started.

"I just want to look at the stars for a bit. Do you know any constellations? The only one I know is the Big Dipper."

Wyatt scooted closer and pointed up at the sky. "Do you see those three bright stars all lined up?"

Harper found them. "I think so."

"That's Orion's belt. If you go straight up from the star on the right, you'll see another bright one. Do you see it? That's the beginning of his arm, which stretches out this way and is holding his bow for hunting. See that line of five stars? They curve just like a bow."

"I see it. That is so cool."

"A couple years ago, I was on a cattle drive in Colorado and there was this guy who would have been Mr. Littlejohn's favorite student. He knew all about the stars and all the stories behind the constellations. He'd pick a couple out every night and tell us all about them. It was actually something to look forward to in the evenings."

"I like that you paid attention and learned something." That was one thing they had in common. They were both curious and willing to try new things.

"Ah, so you're into smart guys, is that it? Here I thought I had to be manly and tough to keep your interest."

Harper giggled. "Oh, I'm searching for a smart, tough, manly man who has a bit of an artistic side. Know anyone that well-rounded?"

"You're the one in possession of my amazing artwork, are you not?"

"This is true. I am in possession of the one and only Wyatt Blackwell original. I guess you do fit the bill of what I'm looking for."

"Too bad I'm looking for a super famous social media influencer who is not only beautiful but also really good at things like photography and marketing."

Harper could feel her cheeks begin to flush. "Well, I'm not sure if you've noticed..."

"Oh, I forgot to add, she needs to be as talented as I am at painting. If you recall, my gran didn't think your painting was very good."

"Wow." She rolled over and lightly punched his arm. "*You* said mine was better than yours. Did you forget that already?"

Wyatt grabbed her wrist before she could slug him again. "I'm not sure how to feel about this violent streak you have, though. That could be a deal breaker."

His face was close to hers again. She lifted her head just enough that their lips could connect. Wyatt kissed her slow and soft. Harper felt like she could melt right there.

He pulled away and smiled at her. It was more beautiful than all the stars in the sky.

"Wyatt, do you want to have a look at Neptune?" Mr. Littlejohn asked.

"Sounds like it's our turn." Wyatt hopped up and held out a hand to help Harper to her feet.

They each looked through the telescope at the tiny blue planet up in the sky. Harper knew she should have been excited about this part of the adventure but all she could think about was that kiss. So much for keeping expectations low.

CHAPTER THIRTEEN

"CAN I HAVE more bacon?" Olivia asked.

Ryder grabbed a slice for himself and passed the plate to his daughter. "I wish I could make bacon this crispy. I always seem to burn it."

"You're a fire chief who sets fires as well as he puts them out," Nash teased.

"That's why we don't ask you to help with the cooking around here," Corliss said, pouring herself more orange juice.

"For someone who has her own long list of issues in the kitchen, I'm not sure I'd be making fun of anyone else's abilities," Gran reminded her.

Wyatt stifled a laugh. He knew better than to chime in on this one. He finished off the last of his pancakes and took his plate to the sink.

"Where are you headed in such a rush?" Corliss asked like he knew she would.

"It's my day off, isn't it?"

She got that look on her face like she was about to ask him for something he was not going to want to do. "It is, but I thought you might be able to finish working on my car today. Please?"

Wyatt scrubbed his face with his hand. "Sis, I could work on that car today, tomorrow and the rest of my life and it isn't going to run any better than it does right now. That thing is ready to be put out of its misery."

"I tried to tell her," Gran said.

Nash snatched the last blueberry muffin. "We've all tried to tell her."

"Oh, come on, little brother. There's got to be something you can do."

"Maybe it's time to get a new car, sweetheart," Ryder suggested.

"As if we can afford a new car right now. In case you haven't noticed, all of our money is going to save this ranch."

The room fell silent. Gran cleared her throat and pushed her chair back, causing a goose-bump-inducing screech. "No one asked you to throw every last dollar you have into this place. The Flying Spur is my responsibility and I will make sure we pay the loan back on my own if I have to."

"Gran, I didn't mean to—"

Gran raised a hand to stop her from finishing that sentence. "I know you mean well, darlin', but I am not going to leave this world feeling like a burden. That's not the way I want to go out."

"You aren't a burden," Corliss assured her. "I want to save the ranch for all of us just as much as I want to save it for you. We all do."

"She's not wrong, Gran. This place is my home. Where in the world would I go if I wasn't here?" Nash asked.

"I hear what you're saying," Gran said, running a hand over the top of her head. "I need to go lie down for a bit. I'm not feeling my best."

Everyone exchanged anxious looks when she left. Big E stood up from the table. "When you get to be our age, it's hard not to feel like you should be able to do more than you can. Passing the torch is tough. On one hand, you're happy to be done and on the other, you want to believe you could keep going for another eighty years. Delaney wants to know that she's giving you something worth keeping. That she's handing off a blessing not a curse. I understand that better than she knows. My grandsons have done things with my ranch I couldn't have dreamed of, but they weren't always so sure they could pull it off. Given your gran's situation, she needs to know you're going to pull it off."

The old man wandered off to do whatever it was that he did all day. No one really knew. Wyatt felt bad wanting to leave, but Harper was waiting and being with Harper was going to be a lot more fun than trying to prove to Gran they were ready for this challenge.

"I'll look at your car once more later today. I have some plans this afternoon."

"You and your plans. What is going on with you? You never have plans. You don't like anyone in Eagle Springs," Nash said.

"I like plenty of people in Eagle Springs. I like almost everyone sitting at the table right now."

"Almost everyone?" Olivia said with a mouthful of bacon.

"He's teasing your uncle Nash, honey,"

Ryder explained. "You are implying you don't like Nash, right?"

Wyatt chuckled. "Don't worry, Ryder. I like you. Even more than I like Nash."

"Are you still here?" Nash asked with a scowl. "You should go since you said you were going."

Wyatt didn't argue. If they were going to let him escape, he was out of there. He had arranged to take Harper to the hot springs, and honestly, he'd been looking forward to it since she asked to go. Harper had been on his mind so often, he was afraid he'd slip up and say her name out loud in front of everyone.

Worse, when he thought about her, he couldn't stop thinking about that kiss the other night. It wasn't like the ones they shared in Las Vegas. The one on Friday hadn't been about pure physical attraction like those Vegas ones. It had been about a real connection. He had kissed her because there was something happening between them.

It scared him half to death.

It wasn't going to stop him from spending as much time as he could with Harper while he still had the chance. He grabbed his stuff and hopped in his truck.

Harper was waiting outside Brock's house when he pulled up. Her blonde hair was up in a ponytail today and there was a backpack slung over her shoulder and a picnic basket in her hand. She was smiling from ear to ear as she jogged up to the truck.

"Hi!" she said, climbing in next to him. "I brought food to fuel us in case we want to go hiking before or after we take a dip in the springs."

"I sure hope this place is going to live up to your expectations. I'm beginning to feel the pressure to not disappoint you."

"You could never, and Eagle Springs has yet to disappoint. In fact, my mom and I went to this glassblowing demonstration yesterday. It was fascinating. We ended up signing up for a class. You should join us. You get to make a glass pumpkin sculpture. In December, they let you make ornaments for your Christmas tree."

"Where is there a glassblowing studio?"

"It's on this farm just outside of the downtown area. They also sell all these beautiful glass pieces. Decorative sculptures, bowls, vases. Gorgeous artwork. Do you know the Sullivans? They run the place."

"Bruce Sullivan?"

"That was his name. Bruce and Cathy. They were so nice."

"Bruce used to raise prize-winning pigs. Every year they'd come home with a ton of ribbons from the state fair. Bruce used to be my 4-H leader."

"Small town strikes again. There isn't anyone in this town that you don't know. Let me guess—you also went to high school with his daughter Gina?"

Wyatt couldn't help but smile. "She was in my sister Adele's grade. They were friends."

"She was super sweet and when I told her that I was going to the hot springs, she's the one who told me about the hiking and the falls. She said there was a covered bridge on the way. She even made me a little map so I would get the best pictures." She pulled out a sheet of paper from her backpack with a rough drawing scribbled on it.

"Gina is great. Is she working at her parents' glassblowing shop?"

"She runs the gift shop there. She also suggested that we check out the Cranky

Crow, which I remembered from your shirt the other night, so my mom and I went there for lunch. Serena didn't love it, but at least they had one salad on the menu so she could eat. I thought the place was hilarious. Waldo the Wolverine above the bar? The owner told us that Waldo knows all, sees all and hears all. So strange, but I totally love it."

"You met Harriet?"

"Don't worry—I didn't tell her I was married to her best friend's grandson."

Wyatt wasn't worried that she told Harriet anything. He was much more concerned about Harriet and the other people who had met Harper over the last few days talking to each other and putting two and two together that the woman hanging out with Wyatt was also Brock's stepdaughter. Harriet would be sure to share that information with Denny.

After the way Gran reacted to Corliss making an offhanded comment about not being able to afford a car, Wyatt couldn't imagine what she'd do if she found out that he'd been seeing Brock's stepdaughter behind her back.

"You don't always have to say anything to get the town talking about things we don't want them to talk about." He had lost sight of the danger that being seen together around town posed. It was only a matter of time before the family figured things out. The only thing Wyatt had any chance of truly keeping secret was that they were married.

"I'm making things harder for you, aren't I?" All the exuberance she had when she got in the truck evaporated.

"Hey, I'm not going to ask you to hide inside your mother's house the whole time you're here. You have a right to go out and do things, meet people." She started to say something, but he stopped her. "I also know you need to spend some time with me so you can post to your followers online. I made a deal with you and I plan to stick to my word."

Harper visibly relaxed in the seat. "I appreciate that more than I can tell you. How do I make this less complicated for you, though? You literally know everyone. There's nowhere I can go in this town that there aren't people who know you. Everyone knows you."

Those were the facts. There was only one solution. "I don't think we can keep knowing each other a secret much longer. My gran is going to hear about Brock's stepdaughter being in town. She's going to eventually hear that I was seen with Brock's stepdaughter either at the art studio or Eagle Ridge or later today at the hot springs. People are going to talk and sooner than later they will make the connection."

"So what do we do about it?"

"We're going to have to come clean about knowing each other. I have to introduce you to the rest of the family and tell Gran you're Brock's stepdaughter."

"Your gran might be the first person I don't make a good first impression on if you have to tell her that. I don't know what Brock did, but would she really hold it against me?"

"Brock works for the bank that called in the loan on our ranch. No one knows why the bank would suddenly want to cut ties with the Blackwells, seeing that we have been one of the longest-running businesses in town."

"She's mad at Brock for making her switch banks?"

Wyatt shook his head. "There's no bank in a hundred miles willing to give us a loan on our land, which is also awfully suspicious, but it's the main reason Gran is so mad at Brock. We're determined to pay off the loan so we don't owe anyone. That's why I'm here. I'm doing the work of three ranch hands, so we could cut expenses way down. Each one of us grandkids is doing something to get enough money to pay it back."

"Isn't the ranch profitable enough to help you pay off the loan?"

Wyatt wasn't sure where to begin to explain all the things that had gone wrong lately to eat up all the profits the ranch had made. "We've had setback after setback. Gran's been sick, real sick. My parents recently retired and took a buyout for their piece of the ranch. We sold some of the cattle to try to stay afloat but at the same time, we lost a bunch of horses due to disease. The money just dried up at the absolute worst time for Brock to decide to call in the bank note."

"I'm so sorry. I didn't realize how bad things were."

How could she know? This was private family business. "We're Blackwells. We'll figure it out. My brothers and sisters, we're all working together to get the money. When we work as a team, nothing can stop us."

"Now I'm back to being jealous of that big family of yours."

He put his hand on hers. "You ready to meet my whole family? Even if they aren't all nice to you right away?"

"If they had anything to do with why you are the man you are, they can't be all that bad."

He gave her hand a squeeze. "Let's hope so."

WYATT HADN'T BEEN to the hot springs since he was a teenager and his group of friends came out here to celebrate after graduation. He'd never taken the hike to the falls. Harper sure had a way of making Eagle Springs seem new to him.

"There's the covered bridge," Harper said as they approached it. "Can you pull over? This is the cutest place to take pictures."

The Bennett Road Covered Bridge had seen better days. The red exterior was a bit faded and the white trim was peeling. The shaker-style roof needed to be patched in more than one place. Wooden letters spelled out the name of the bridge above the entrance. The *G* was missing, so it currently said Bennett Road Bride. Harper didn't seem to mind one bit.

"Can you take a photo of me if I set it up for you? And then maybe we could set the phone on the truck to get one of both of us?"

It didn't seem too special to Wyatt, but Harper was sure to make it charming once she got done working her magic on her photographs. Wyatt did as he was instructed and took a couple shots of Harper standing in the middle of the entrance in various poses.

"I bet people take wedding photos here all the time," she said, coming over to check his work.

"You're asking the wrong guy about that. I don't know what people do at weddings. I don't even remember what I did at my own."

Harper tried and failed to not laugh. "Yeah, well, that's why I filmed the whole thing, so we could see how ridiculous we were and relive the embarrassment over and over."

Since there was no traffic coming in either direction, she had Wyatt park the truck right in front of the bridge. She got him in position and then set up her phone. Once everything was ready, she pressed a button on her screen and ran over to him.

"Look at me like you don't regret telling Elvis you'd take me as your wife until death do us part."

Wyatt didn't have an ounce of regret in him at the moment. He wished they hadn't gotten themselves in this mess, but this mess brought this incredible woman into his life. How could he regret that?

Harper went back and forth between him and her phone four or five times. The last one she warned him ahead of time, "I'm going to kiss you, Cowboy Wyatt. I hope you're ready."

He'd been waiting to kiss her since he dropped her off Friday night. She set the timer and ran over to him, jumping into his arms and wrapping her legs around his waist. She smelled like sunscreen and lavender. It was fitting because she was like sunshine and flowers—colorful and warm. She laughed and then kissed him. He didn't care if the camera was done shooting, he kept kissing her until they were both startled by a honking car horn.

Wyatt set her down and waved an apology to the people sitting in the car idling behind his truck. Harper grabbed her phone off the hood and they both jumped in the truck.

"Whoops," she said through her giggles.

"We are terrible at being discreet."

"Good thing we're telling your family about me soon."

"We'll be lucky if they don't know by the time I can get to them."

"Fine, no more kissing pictures."

"I didn't say that." He snuck a glance her way to see her reaction.

Her smile was luminous. "Because they're the most popular pictures that I post?"

"Right. Because they are the most popular. No other reason."

Wyatt was in over his head with this woman, but he couldn't stop himself. *Enjoy it while it lasts*, he told himself. This feeling had an expiration date.

CHAPTER FOURTEEN

HARPER CLOSED HER EYES and let her other senses enjoy the High Creek Falls. There was something about the sound of running water that was so relaxing. These weren't like the waterfalls she'd seen in Hawaii that were hidden away in the lush rainforests of Maui, but they were unique in their own way. She took a deep breath and inhaled the fresh scent in the air. The towering pine trees that surrounded the falls were so fragrant. She opened her eyes and watched the water turn white as it bounced and scattered down the rocky side of the cliff. All of this was backdropped by the bluest sky she'd ever seen.

"I can't believe I never came up here before." Somehow Wyatt had never bothered to visit the falls in all his years living in Eagle Springs. Harper loved watching him discover something new in a place he thought he knew so well.

"I have been to many places in this big, wide world, and this is turning out to be one of my favorites. I don't know why I didn't notice how much Eagle Springs had to offer when I was here for my mom's wedding. I think I was in such shock that I didn't even try to see the good here."

Wyatt picked up a fallen twig and tossed it aside. "I can see how it might have been a bit of a culture shock. Wyoming is not like California."

"At least not the part of California that I'm from. Not that I'm home much these days. I don't even know that I'd call my apartment back in LA a home."

"I know you travel for your job, but you've always lived in California, haven't you?"

"Most of the time. We bounced around a lot depending on who Serena was dating or married to at the moment."

"Was Brock the first guy your mom married who wasn't from California?"

Harper had to think about it for a minute. Some of her mom's relationships were so short-lived that she barely remembered them. There was one time they had to move out of state. "Larry Stevens lived in Santa Monica but got transferred to Phoenix when they were still married. We moved with him and four months later, they were divorced and Mom and I were back in LA. Serena did not like living in the desert."

"It had to be hard having no control as a kid over where you lived or who you lived with. All that change all the time had to be hard."

Harper didn't like to think about herself as a helpless kid. She tried to remember the good times because if she dwelled on the bad, she might get stuck feeling sorry for herself.

"It was challenging at times for sure. I definitely never knew how things would end, but I always knew they would eventually. That helped when I didn't like the guy very much. At least I knew he wouldn't be around forever. It was sad when I thought things were good. I knew they wouldn't last."

"What about now? Do you think your mom and Brock have a chance at forever?"

Given Serena's track record, Brock's

chances of keeping her were low. "Let's just say that there's a reason I'm so invested in making Eagle Springs a little more Serena-friendly."

If Serena and Brock were going to stay together, Harper's mom needed to feel like she belonged here. It wasn't impossible, but it would take some time.

Harper got one more picture of the falls. Serena would love this view. Maybe they could come back one day, meditate by the falls and go for a dip in the hot springs. It would be similar to a spa day without having to pay a dime.

"I have to admit, you've been making Eagle Springs a bit more Wyatt-friendly," Wyatt confessed as they made their way back down the trail.

"Have I?" Harper folded and unfolded the map in her hands.

"All the other times I've been home, I've been focused on where I was going next and how quickly I could get there. This time, I've been thinking more about what you and I can do next around here."

Harper was overjoyed by that. She wasn't the only one obsessing over the idea of spending more time together. Harper checked her map for the spot Gina had marked as the best picnic place. As they came around the bend, there was the spot— a small, flat patch of grass that offered awesome views of the falls. She took off her backpack to get the blanket she'd brought for them to have their picnic on.

"This is it. Are you ready for some food?"

Wyatt set down the picnic basket that he so graciously offered to carry. "You have successfully helped me work up an appetite. I'm starving."

Harper opened the basket and laid out the goodies she had chosen. "I picked up some meats and cheeses at the deli downtown. They said that the cheese is made at one of the local dairy farms. I tried a sample—it was delicious."

Wyatt wasn't shy. He helped himself to some of the salami and pepperonis. Harper handed him a cracker with a slice of the farm fresh sharp cheddar cheese. He gobbled it right up.

He took a swig of water to wash it all down. "I've decided that I should take you with me wherever I go from now on," he said as he wiped his mouth with the back of his hand. "You have this incredible knack for finding what makes a town great."

He was having a hard time understanding that this was what she did. It was how she made a living. She went places to discover why other people would want to go there, too.

"It's almost like I should go places and try things and post about it on my social media accounts. Maybe people would be interested in that."

Wyatt narrowed his eyes at her. "Are you calling me Captain Obvious?"

Harper scrunched up her nose. "Kind of."

"I get it. You do this all the time. I'm complimenting you on your ability to dust places off and find what makes them shine. You are good at what you do even when you aren't doing it for a job."

"Well, I am sort of learning about Eagle Springs for a job. Remember when I told you I have the opportunity to stay here a little longer?"

"Yeah." Wyatt popped another cracker covered in cheese into his mouth.

"I'm hoping to be part of a project that's

going to take what's great about Eagle Springs and build on it. I think this could be a place that people want to come and visit. Somewhere they'll spend money and help the town grow and prosper."

"You'd have a lot of support in town for that. It also sounds like the perfect job for you."

She was happy to hear him say that. Hopefully Xavier would agree and use some of her ideas. "I hope I get a chance to be a part of it. This place is growing on me."

"My gran will love that you appreciate what Eagle Springs has to offer. There's no one who loves this town more than my grandmother. She has worked her whole life to make this place somewhere the community can be proud to call home."

Anything that could help her get in good with Denny Blackwell was a positive. Harper would be sure to mention all the things she'd fallen in love with thus far. Harper wondered how the elder Blackwell would feel about her being in love with her grandson. She might have to leave that out for now. Saying something like that out loud would make her feel too vulnerable.

They finished eating what she had packed and took a few selfies with the falls in the background. These posts were going to garner the most likes yet. She slipped her backpack on and retied her shoe.

She popped back up and started down the trail. "Last one to the hot springs has to buy the other one a drink at the Cranky Crow."

Wyatt, clearly caught off guard, almost forgot the picnic basket and had to go back. Harper thought she had the easy win, but just before she got to the circle of rocks that lined the outer edge of the geothermally-heated pool, Wyatt flew past her and celebrated like a prize-winning fighter does in the ring after a knockout.

"You're lucky I'm a simple beer man and not an expensive whiskey drinker. Your tab should be reasonable."

Harper had her bathing suit under her clothes. She quickly kicked off her shoes and stripped off her shorts and shirt. "Did I say last one *to* the springs or last one *in* the springs? I think I said in."

A stunned Wyatt stood frozen on the edge as Harper ran into the gravel-bottom pool, splashing him on her way. When he finally came to his senses, he protested. "You said to. You did not say in. I won fair and square."

Harper sank down until she was submerged up to her neck. The steam rose off the water. "I can't remember. We're going to have to call it a tie. Are you coming or not?"

Wyatt grabbed the hem of his shirt and pulled it up over his head. Harper had to look away. Shirtless Wyatt was only going to raise her heart rate when the purpose of being there was to unwind.

He joined her in the water, splashing her when he got close enough.

"Hey!"

"You said to not in and you know it."

"Fine," she said with a smirk. "I said to. You won. I'll buy you a beer."

"Thank you for being honest. You had me scared there for a second that I couldn't trust you."

"You can trust me, Wyatt," she assured him. It mattered that he trusted her because he was becoming her person. The one who she needed to believe in her.

He found her hand underwater and intertwined their fingers. They were good. This, whatever it was between them, was good.

Soaking in the hot springs was the perfect way to spend some time after hiking to the falls. Surrounded by tree-covered mountains, Harper had more pictures than she needed to show off the absolute beauty of this place. Not only was she falling in love with Wyatt Blackwell but with Eagle Springs as well.

"I can feel my muscles thanking me for coming here," she said with her eyes closed.

"It is pretty amazing," Wyatt said. "I forgot what this was like. I should come here every time I'm home visiting. I haven't felt this relaxed in forever."

Harper couldn't agree more. "This was a good day."

Wyatt hummed in agreement.

"We should probably get back to reality, though."

Wyatt groaned in disagreement.

"Maybe we can go home, clean up, you can introduce me to the family?"

This time, Wyatt was quiet. She wasn't sure if that meant he thought that was a good idea or not.

"Should we do that another day?" she asked.

Wyatt stood up and climbed out of the

water. He found his backpack and pulled out a towel. "I'm ready if you're ready."

That was a loaded question. She liked the idea of getting to know the people who loved Wyatt. She was also terrified they would reject her. Was she ready for that possibility?

"I trust you, so I'm ready."

SERENA AND BROCK were watching television when Harper got back to the house to get ready for the big meet and greet with the Blackwells.

"How was your date?" Serena asked, not looking away from the screen.

Brock, on the other hand, turned around. "Date? Who did you have a date with?"

"It was not a date. I went out on a hike with Wyatt."

"Not a date," her mother repeated with a laugh. "Brock is cooking rainbow trout for dinner."

"I'm actually going to Wyatt's after I shower and clean up."

"You're going to have dinner with the Blackwells?" Brock asked, causing Harper to stop.

"I'm a little nervous about it. Wyatt told

me about how your bank called in their loan and that's why his grandma is mad at you. I don't know why she's holding it against you like it was personal."

Brock was on his feet. "Denny Blackwell is a stubborn, angry old woman. She thinks she's the only one who can make a difference in this town. She'll see that when she's gone, Eagle Springs will be fine, better than fine."

"When she's gone? You mean because she's sick?"

"No. I mean when she has to sell the ranch. What do you mean she's sick?"

Harper realized that she may have shared information that wasn't public knowledge. She tried to deflect. "I really don't have any information about what's happening. I only know she's not going to sell the ranch. That's why Wyatt is here. They are all doing what they need to do to pay off the loan." Again, she tried to head for the bedroom.

"Wyatt's here to do what?" Brock asked, interrupting her retreat. "How in the world can the Blackwells come up with enough money to pay off their debts?"

"Like I said, I don't know exactly. Wyatt's here to work. He said he replaced some ranch hands that they had to let go. I have no idea what the others have planned—Wyatt just said all the grandkids were going to do their part to cover it."

Brock was overly interested. "The grandkids are raising the money?"

"It's their ranch, too, right?" she replied, trying to exit the conversation.

"I guess it's a good thing Wyatt is here. If he wasn't here or had to leave, they wouldn't be able to keep things going like they are, huh?"

Harper could feel her forehead wrinkle. "I guess. Listen, I would *love* to talk to you more about things I don't know much about, but I really need to get in the shower," she said, hoping her sarcasm wasn't too caustic.

"Yeah, go. Shower." Brock had his phone in hand and was typing furiously. "You need to get ready for your dinner with the Blackwells."

Harper got ready and once again was paralyzed when it came to finding the perfect outfit. First impressions were her strength, but this wasn't simply impressing Wyatt or his young nieces and nephew. This was his tough-as-nails grandmother. Harper needed to look just right.

"Are you doing this again?" Serena stood in the doorway. "Do you need help?"

"Please," Harper said in an exhale.

Serena began choosing articles of clothing from the discard pile on the floor. "You must really like this guy if you get this anxious every time you go out together."

"I want to make the right impression when I meet his family. They aren't like the people I usually surround myself with. I don't want them to take one look at me and dismiss me as an entitled, superficial California millennial."

"If they do, that says a lot more about them than it does you. You are an intelligent and kind young woman who might not plow fields or rope horses or whatever they do, but you are as hardworking as they come. It will be their loss if they don't want to know you."

Harper put her hand over her heart. It wasn't like Serena to be so generous with the compliments. "Aw. Thanks, Mom."

"Just remember they aren't so different from us. They have hopes and dreams. They get hurt and they feel joy. They want to be accepted and loved. Just like us."

Someone had been listening. These were the same things Harper had been trying to tell her mother all week. If she wanted to make Eagle Springs her home, she had to at least try to connect with someone other than Brock in this community.

"So what you're saying is I should take my own advice?"

"You thought it was good enough to give—I assume that means it's good enough to take." She placed a sweater and a pair of leggings on the bed. "You should wear your hair up and the necklace with the big *H*, because you are Harper Hayes and proud of it."

Harper startled her mother by throwing her arms around her and giving her a hug. "I love you, Mom."

Serena relaxed into the embrace and hugged Harper back. "I love you, too, sweetheart."

It had been a long time since Harper felt this close to her mom. Coming to Eagle Springs might have been the blessing of a lifetime. If Harper did decide to settle down someday, she could see herself being here, close to her mom and near Wyatt's home base.

She got changed and fixed her hair. She stared at herself in the mirror and repeated back the same affirmations her mom had given her. She was an intelligent and kind woman. If they rejected her, that said more about them than her.

Her phone buzzed with a notification. Her heart sank as she read the text from Wyatt.

You can't come over tonight. She knows.

CHAPTER FIFTEEN

GRAN WAS SITTING in the rocking chair on the front porch. A man Wyatt didn't recognize stood in front of her. Good thing Wyatt had shown up at the house when he had that evening. She had a piece of paper in her hand and looked like she wanted to send the guy packing.

"I don't know where you get your information, Mr. Howard, but we're doing just fine and I am not planning on kicking the bucket anytime soon. You can take your offer and you can throw it in that wheelbarrow by the barn with the rest of the manure."

"Ms. Blackwell, I am simply trying to do you a favor. I am going to buy this property. I thought you might like to have some money to leave behind for your family, but if you want me to give it to the bank, then so be it."

"I know you aren't from around here, so

I'll excuse your ignorance and misguided bravado. Just know, I have been here since before you were born and the Flying Spur will still be here long after you are gone. Good night, Mr. Howard."

The city slicker in his khaki pants and fancy loafers sneered at Gran. "We'll see about that."

"I believe it's time for you to go," Wyatt said, climbing up onto the porch, feeling protective of his grandmother. Denny Blackwell had no problem standing her ground, but this guy could not take a hint.

The guy put up his hands and backed away and down the steps. "I'm going to give you to the end of the month to decide. But come October first, this deal will be gone forever. I hope you don't leave this world with any regrets."

"Do you go away with the deal? Because that sounds like something I can get behind," Gran quipped.

The man retreated to his luxury black sedan with Colorado plates.

"Who was that?" Wyatt asked as he watched the man drive away.

"That was someone very interested in buying my ranch."

Gran had never considered selling her land, so it was strange that someone would come looking for a deal. "Why would he think you wanted to sell the ranch?"

"Good question. He already made an offer. Sent me something almost right after the loan was called in. It was like he was told we were in financial trouble."

"How would he know that?"

"Another good question. Want to know what really caught my attention tonight? He seemed to be aware of a lot of things that he shouldn't." Gran folded the piece of paper with Mr. Howard's offer on it in half and then ripped it into tiny pieces.

"Like what?"

"Come sit here with me." She nodded toward the other empty rocker. Wyatt did as he was told. "All week, the same name has been coming up over and over. First, it was Regina Timmons gossiping with her friend about a new woman in town. Then I heard Pete Roberts talking about how he was hoping that this woman wasn't just visiting because he was going to ask her out. I didn't think much of it until I went into town today to see Harriet. She told me she finally met Brock Bedford's new wife. Said she was one of these West Coast types. Wanted to know if anything on the menu was organic."

Wyatt knew what was coming next. He thought about beating her to the punch but chickened out. He swallowed his confession down.

Denny kept going. "Harriet also said Brock's stepdaughter was there, too. Visiting from California. Real pretty. Full of questions about the Cranky Crow, the other businesses in town. She wanted to know what Harriet thought made Eagle Springs somewhere people would want to visit."

Typical Harper, doing what she does best—getting the inside scoop from those in the know. "Gran."

"Well, turns out this young lady was the same person I'd been hearing about all week. Her name is…ah…" Gran squeezed her eyes shut and snapped her fingers "…what's her name?"

"Harper," Wyatt said barely above a whisper.

Gran's eyes flew open and she pointed a

finger at him. "That's right. Harper. On my way back to my truck, I bumped into Jill Kiehn, which surprised me because part of me thought you were running off today to go spend some time with your old friend Jill. We talked about how you had been to her painting class. She mentioned that Harper was there, too. In fact, she specifically said you and Harper were there together."

"Harper is my friend. She's the woman the kids and Levi were introduced to at Tucker's the first night I was in town. She and I met by chance in Vegas."

"She's your friend? You just happened to become friends with Brock Bedford's step-daughter in Las Vegas right after he called in my loan? Right after I turned down some guy who offered to buy my ranch?"

Wyatt didn't like what she was insinuating. "Gran, Harper has nothing to do with Brock and whatever is going on with the ranch. She's here visiting her mom."

"Did you tell your friend I was sick?"

Wyatt opened his mouth only to close it. He had told Harper she was sick. "There's no reason why Harper would tell anyone anything. And if she did repeat something I said to her, it was done so innocently. There's no way she's sending some guy to your house to pressure you into selling."

"Brock Bedford is up to something. I don't know what, but I'm going to find out." Gran rose out of the chair. "In the meantime, I suggest you be a bit more careful about the company you keep."

Wyatt sat there while she went inside. How could Harper have anything to do with this? There was no way she knew who he was when they met in Las Vegas. She had no idea what was going on between Brock and Gran.

Yet, how could this Mr. Howard know about Denny being sick? Why would he come over tonight, the same day that Wyatt told Harper his gran was sick, and try to use that against her? He didn't like this. He hated doubting her.

There would be no introduction tonight. Harper was not going to be welcomed at Gran's dinner table after what just happened. He sent Harper a quick text telling her not to come over. He couldn't talk to her right now. He had to get his head on straight.

There were a lot of ways someone could

have figured out Gran was sick. How many times had he said there were no secrets in a small town? Someone could have overheard Gran's close friends talking about it. Maybe they saw her going to dialysis. Maybe they just noticed she'd been looking a bit worn out lately. It was quite possible Mr. Howard had no idea she was sick and was only making a lucky guess.

Harper was not trying to help anyone take the Flying Spur away from his family. He couldn't believe that. He'd prove it to everyone, especially his grandmother.

"How's it going, young man?" Big E eased his way up the porch steps.

"It's been better."

"Sorry to hear that. Anything I can do to help?"

Wyatt was going to say no, until something told him to stop. His great-uncle was here to aid Gran. He was bound and determined to figure out who had it out for her. If there was anyone who could help him prove that Harper wasn't the one behind all this, it was Big E.

"Actually, I think you are the only one who can help me right now."

Big E didn't or maybe couldn't hide his surprise. "You have no idea how exciting it is to hear that. Not because I want you to have a problem," he clarified. "It's not often my family lets me come to the rescue willingly. How can I lend a hand?"

WYATT FELT GOOD about joining forces with his uncle Elias. The old man wasn't afraid to go hunting for the truth wherever it was hiding. Since Wyatt had another long to-do list waiting for him come morning, he was trusting Big E to be his eyes and ears.

"Is there a reason why you look like someone offered you soggy waffles for breakfast?" Corliss asked on Monday. They were working together to round up the calves in the herd to start the weaning process. This wasn't something Wyatt could do alone.

"I don't look like that."

"How would you know what you look like right now? I'm looking at you. I can see your face. I know what you look like. You look like someone who is not happy with the way his morning is going. Did something happen that I'm not aware of?"

"I'm fine. I don't know what you're talking about."

"Wouldn't have anything to do with Gran finding out that you've been secretly dating Brock Bedford's stepdaughter, would it?"

Wyatt swung his head in her direction. "How do you know about that?"

"Have you been away from Eagle Springs so long that you forgot how information spreads faster than a forest fire around here?"

Wyatt shook his head in frustration. "I didn't realize you were into small-town gossip."

Corliss threw her head back and laughed. "Don't try to turn this on me. Ryder's the one who heard you were making out with some mystery woman at the astronomy club meeting last week."

Wyatt knew that was going to come back to haunt him. "Stupid astronomy club," he grumbled.

"I am not going to ask why you were at that meeting because I want to save that story for a day when I need a good laugh."

"I'm never telling you that story."

"Fine. Well, back to my story. Yesterday,

Mason heard Gran talking about someone named Harper, and he reminded me
that Harper was the name of the woman
you introduced to everyone at Tucker's. It
didn't seem like much of a leap to assume
that Harper from Tucker's was the mystery
woman you were making out with. Then,
Adele called me this morning and said that
she talked to Gina Sullivan this weekend
and Gina told her that she met Brock's new
wife and stepdaughter, who also happens to
be named Harper. It was pretty easy to put
it together that Gran isn't too happy that you
are sleeping with the enemy."

Wyatt's temper flared. It was one thing to
tease him; it was another to point fingers at
Harper. "First of all, I am not sleeping with
anyone. Secondly, Harper is not the enemy.
Anyone who knows her would never think
of her as anyone's enemy. She's not like that.
If you met her, you would see that she's one
of the nicest people you've probably ever
met, and I don't appreciate people assum-
ing things about her before they have even
exchanged two words with her."

"Take a breath, Wyatt." Corliss gave her
horse a nudge to speed up to get side by

side with him. "I didn't mean to make you mad. I was joking around. I don't really understand what Gran is thinking right now, but we all know anyone remotely associated with Brock is going to be caught in her crosshairs. It doesn't mean they deserve to be. I'm sure that Harper is a perfectly nice person. She must be if you're ready to bite my head off for mentioning her."

"You did more than mention her, Corliss." He wasn't going to let her get away with pretending she didn't call Harper the enemy. "You insinuated that she was one of the bad guys. Gran might lump everyone who has a relationship with Brock in the same group, but I would hope you and everyone else could see that if someone knows Brock, it doesn't mean they are against us."

His big sister stayed quiet for a few seconds. Hopefully, she would take what he said to heart and lay off Harper. He'd much rather she gave him a hard time for going to an astronomy club meeting than accuse Harper of the same things Gran did.

"I'm sorry. I didn't realize your feelings for this woman were so strong. We are talking about the woman you met less than two weeks ago, right?"

Wyatt adjusted the hat on his head. The sun was beating down on them causing the sweat to run along the sides of his face and wet the back of his neck. His feelings were intense and unexplainable. "Can we talk about something else? I will literally talk to you about anything else."

"Fine. Consider this topic dropped," Corliss said. "For now." She whistled for Bow to help them round up the cattle. That dog was no shepherd but he sure thought he was.

Wyatt zigzagged in a wide arc behind the herd to get them moving in the direction they wanted. He reminded Corliss not to stay in any of the cattle's blindspots for too long. That caused them to get stressed and more difficult to control.

Once they got the herd in the corral, they went to work separating the calves from the cows. It was no easy task. Calves didn't like being away from their mamas. Mamas weren't big fans of having their calves taken away either. They managed it and the two groups were separated by a sturdy fence so the calves couldn't nurse anymore but wouldn't be as stressed because they could be nose to nose with the mothers.

"You know I've worked on a couple ranches where they put a nose ring on the calves to prevent them from nursing instead of fence weaning," Wyatt said to Corliss as they dismounted their horses. "They get to stay with their mom and I can attest to the fact that it causes a lot less stress. At this one ranch in New Mexico, there was no bawling. The calves walked less and ate more when they were finally separated."

"How much does something like that cost? And how many times do you have to run the calves through the chute? Twice? That's a lot more labor."

Everything was about money these days. How could Wyatt have forgotten? "I'm not saying it's something we have to do, but maybe once we get back on our feet, it's something to look at. You have to worry way less about the calves' health that way. There's pros and cons to both methods. I just thought you might want to know what other ranches are doing."

"Huh, maybe if you decided to stick

around, we could work together to get this place running in tip-top shape."

Wyatt loosened the strap on the saddle. He was here to help temporarily. It was never meant to be a permanent thing. He knew his family wished he felt differently. They were happy here, well, maybe not all of them. Levi's injury had forced him off the road. Instead of traveling the rodeo circuit, he was stuck in Eagle Springs. Wyatt didn't have anything or anyone holding him there.

"You're the right person to run the ranch, Corliss. You don't need me. You and Nash will have everything under control once we get the loan paid off."

"We can always use an experienced foreman. Someone who keeps up with the latest trends in the ranching world. It would also be nice if that person was someone I trusted."

Wyatt lifted the saddle off his horse. It was sweet of her to act like he was somehow necessary, but they didn't *need* him. Hiring a reliable foreperson wouldn't be impossible.

"I believe you will find that person. I'm not so sure it's me."

Nash walked into the tack room where

they were cleaning up the horses. "Uh, Wyatt, you might want to come out here. Somebody's come by to see you and I think you better get them the heck away before Gran catches sight of them."

Corliss offered to finish up with the horses. Wyatt followed Nash expecting Harper to be outside the paddock only to find Brock nervously waiting for him.

Brock slipped off his sunglasses. "Wyatt, we need to talk."

"What are you doing here?" Wyatt asked, his eyes darting around to check for Gran or Uncle Elias.

"I need to talk to you about my step-daughter."

Wyatt guided him back toward his car. They could have a very brief conversation about Harper and then Brock needed to leave. "Is Harper okay?"

"She's…fine. Did she call you?"

Wyatt pinched his brows together. "No, why?" He pulled out his phone to make sure he hadn't missed a call while he was working. There was nothing. "Is something wrong?"

"I just want you to know that I know."

"You know what?"

"I know."

Wyatt had an idea of what he was referring to, but he wasn't going to say anything until Brock said the words. "You know what?"

Brock groaned and pulled his hands out of his pockets. "I know that you and Harper got married. I know that if your grandmother finds out that you've been keeping a secret that big, she will disown you. I know that you are here to keep this dying ranch up and running."

That was more than he expected him to know. Wyatt was thrown a bit off guard. "Harper told you all that?"

"Harper tells me everything. She and I have the same goal to do what's best for our family. If you were smart, you would see that prolonging the demise of the Flying Spur isn't what's best for your family. I know your grandmother has an offer from someone willing to buy this place for good money. Money you all could use to help you do whatever it is you want to do with your lives. If you really care about your family and your grandmother, you will convince her to take that offer."

Brock was obviously in cahoots with whoever that guy was who showed up last night. The guy who knew that their loan had been called in and that Gran was sick. Things he could have known because Brock and Harper told him so.

Wyatt felt like steam was coming out of his ears. "You don't get to come here, of all places, and tell me what's best for my family. You have no say in what's best for my family. Your last name isn't Blackwell."

"My stepdaughter's last name is Blackwell. I'm sure the rest of the family would love to know that."

Wyatt stepped into Brock's personal space and puffed out his chest. "Are you threatening me? You think you have some power here because you know about something that's going to be over as soon as we file some papers in court? My annulment will cut all ties between me and Harper."

Saying it aloud made it hurt more than he expected. Wyatt wasn't ready to accept that Harper couldn't be part of his life.

"Have you thought about what impact

your deceit will have on Denny? Can you imagine what that added stress will do to her when she's already so compromised?"

Wyatt grabbed the front of Brock's shirt. "Do not talk about my grandmother or her health. She could take you down without breaking a sweat."

Brock pushed him away and straightened his shirt. "You need to get that temper in check, young man. I've been known to call the police when assaulted. You should also think long and hard about what I'm telling you. This ranch is going under. If you drag it out, you are going to take years off your grandmother's life. From what I've heard, she doesn't have any years to give."

Wyatt pointed at Brock's car. "You need to get out of here before I call the police and have you arrested for trespassing. Don't come back here either. You are not welcome. That's something everyone in my family is on the same page about."

Brock didn't push his luck. He got in his car and took off. Wyatt was breathing heavy. He needed to cool off before he spoke to either of his siblings. He stalked off to take a break in Betty. He couldn't believe Brock had the nerve to come here and make threats. He also was struggling to understand why Harper told Brock they were married.

They had both agreed not to tell anyone in their families about what happened. They had talked about it more than once. At no time had Harper been unclear about the contentious relationship between Brock and Gran. She had to know that telling Brock anything would have led to trouble. Did she not care? Was she working with Brock to force Gran to sell the ranch?

CHAPTER SIXTEEN

"OUR COFFEE COMES leaded or unleaded and either black or with cream or sugar. I don't even know what a latte is, sweetheart." The waitress tapped her pencil on the order pad in her hand.

Harper had known better than to ask. "I'll just have a regular coffee, but can I get milk instead of cream?"

"You want a glass of milk and a cup of coffee?" the waitress asked.

"Sure." At this point it was easier to go with the flow than try to explain what she wanted. Add a coffee shop with a knowledgeable barista to the list of things that the new and improved Eagle Springs needed when it was refreshed and revived.

The waitress jotted that down and went to get the drinks. Harper checked the door. Brock had told her Xavier wanted to meet with them at nine o'clock sharp Monday morning. Unfortunately, Brock had to check in at the bank first, so he sent her to the diner to greet Xavier on her own.

Harper needed this meeting to go well. After being rejected by the Blackwells last night, it was important to her to do what she could to prove to Mrs. Blackwell that she was more like her than she thought. Harper wanted to bring new businesses to Eagle Springs. She also wanted to draw attention to the wonderful businesses that already existed. Her idea was to keep the charm and simply add to it.

The waitress came back to the booth with her coffee and her glass of milk. "Anything else I can get you while you wait for the rest of your party?"

"No, I'm good. Thank you." Harper waited until she walked away to pour some of the milk into her coffee cup.

The diner was fairly crowded this morning. She was beginning to recognize people from around town. One of the old men at the counter made eye contact. She tried to remember where she had seen him before. Xavier appeared out of nowhere and said her name, causing her to spill some milk on the table.

She grabbed a napkin from the holder and cleaned up her mess. "Xavier."

He slid into the seat across from her. "I didn't mean to startle you. How are you this morning?"

"Happy to be meeting with you. Brock had to take care of something at work and then he's going to join us."

He picked up one of the menus. "What's good here? Anything?" He made a face like he doubted this place made things he'd find edible.

"I'm sure there's something delicious. Maybe a little greasy, but I'd bet it all tastes good."

"When this project goes through, we won't have to worry about finding places to eat that meet the standards of people like you and me."

Harper took a sip of her coffee and tried to make sense of what that meant exactly. "I just want you to know that I am so excited about hearing what you and your company have planned and share with you some of my ideas. We have such an excellent opportunity to put Eagle Springs on the map."

"You mean Mountain Ridge," he said just as the waitress came over to ask him if he wanted anything to drink.

Everything coming out of Xavier's mouth was confusing. She took another gulp of coffee. Maybe she needed more caffeine to help her pay better attention.

As soon as the waitress walked away, in came Brock like a hurricane. "I'm so sorry I'm late." He glared at Harper until she moved over to make room for him to sit down. "I'm looking forward to hearing what you can share with us. Hopefully, we've proven ourselves useful so far."

"Well, I wish I could say that your insider information had convinced someone to get on board with the grand plan, but that's not what happened. I gave her until the end of the month to decide. Maybe she'll come to her senses by then."

The coffee was doing nothing to help this conversation make sense. Harper felt like she was missing several pieces of this puzzle.

"You already talked to her?" Brock asked.

"Went over there last night after I heard from you. Figured why wait. I thought maybe showing up like that would show her how serious I was about it."

"She's a stubborn one," Brock said, clearly understanding what Xavier was talking about. "I respect the sense of urgency, but you might just have to stick to the original plan. Let the time run out and then she has no say."

"I'm usually a patient man, but I have a boss who wants things done sooner than later. It is imperative that we get that deal done. Without that land, we can't move forward with the rest of it."

"I would love to know what the rest of the plan is. Harper has some great ideas she'd like to share as well. We're all in if you'll let us be."

The waitress returned with Xavier's hot tea and offered to take everyone's order.

"Eating here is actually the last thing we want to do. We'll let you know if we need you."

Xavier's rude behavior not only offended the waitress but Harper as well. This meeting was very different from the last. As much as Harper wanted to do something special for the town, she was beginning to worry Mr. Howard wasn't the right partner.

"So, about the rest of the plan…" Brock said, restarting the conversation.

"I was just about to tell Harper when you walked in. Picture this—a mountain resort with all the amenities in the middle of the most picture perfect town. To get there you have to drive down an old-fashioned Main Street filled with a mixture of amazing restaurants and boutique shopping experiences. Everything would be high-end. We want to lure some well-known brands as well as have places completely unique to the area so that people have to come to Wyoming to get it."

"It sounds amazing except I hope you plan to highlight some of the incredible businesses that already exist here in Eagle Springs. I made a list of the most charming parts of this town." Harper dug through her bag, looking for her list.

"Oh, we aren't talking about Eagle Springs. I'm talking about Mountain Ridge. *It* is going to be Wyoming's version of Aspen."

Brock's mouth fell agape, and so did

Harper's. They both stared at Xavier, waiting for him to tell them he was kidding.

"Mountain Ridge? What is Mountain Ridge?" Brock asked.

Xavier's sly smile made Harper sick to her stomach. "That's the name of the new town we're going to build about ten miles north of here in the mountains."

"I thought you were working to revitalize Eagle Springs. Brock told me you've been buying up some properties in Eagle Springs. Why would you do that if you're building a town somewhere else?" Harper asked.

"We need Eagle Springs because this valley is where we're going to put our picturesque lake."

Harper couldn't think straight. She felt like she was in the middle of an elaborate prank. She glanced at Brock to gauge his reaction to this absurd news. He appeared equally stunned.

"You're planning to put this place underwater?" Harper lowered her voice so as not to alert anyone else around.

"And we would like to work with you, Harper, to attract many of those luxury brands here. We'd also like you to join our focus group to get a feel for what people like you would want to see and experience in a place like Mountain Ridge."

Brock finally spoke up. "If Harper joins your team, can we be guaranteed property in Mountain Ridge? What's in it for us?"

His unexpected response left Harper reeling. What was in it for them? Why did that matter? Harper couldn't be a part of something that was going to wipe out this entire town. What was he thinking?

"We appreciate all you've been able to do to help us, Brock. If things go the way we expect them to by year's end, I don't see why we wouldn't set you up on a prime piece of real estate in what we hope will be the most sought after neighborhood in the mountain states."

Harper had heard enough. She dug in her purse to find a few bucks to pay for her coffee. She slipped the cash under her mug. "I need to go."

Brock didn't move. "What do you mean you have to go?"

"I need to go. I don't want to be here anymore. I don't want to be part of this deal."

She suppressed the desire to shove him out of the way so she could escape.

"Harper, what are you talking about?" Brock shifted his focus back to Xavier. "Would you excuse us for a second? Let me talk to her. Everything is fine." He slid out of the seat and waited for Harper to do the same.

Harper's mind was made up. It didn't matter what Brock had to say about it. She would not do business with someone who planned to wipe this town off the map, only to be replaced by a giant lake.

She strode to the exit with no desire to speak to Brock, but he grabbed her arm as soon as they hit the sidewalk outside.

"What are you doing? Is this some kind of plan to play hardball? Is there something else you think we can get out of this deal?"

Every time he opened his mouth, she was more appalled. "Are you really okay with destroying this town? Does it matter to you at all that some of the people in Eagle Springs have lived here their entire lives and wouldn't know where else to go? They certainly couldn't afford to live in Mountain Ridge."

"Oh, don't be so dramatic. People aren't as attached to this town as you think. They'll be paid for their land and go find houses in the neighboring towns. It'll be fine."

"It won't be fine. I have met a lot of people who take great pride in where they are from. There isn't a dollar amount that would lure them away."

"Ha! You don't know people very well, then. Everyone has their price."

Harper's anger heated her cheeks. "Not Denny Blackwell. She isn't going to sell her ranch."

Brock frowned and narrowed his eyes. "Denny Blackwell isn't going to have a choice. She isn't going to be able to stay even if she wants to."

"You're wrong. Her family is going to make sure they stay put."

"By letting go of their ranch hands and counting on Wyatt to do all the work keeping that place running? It's not going to happen."

Harper started putting two and two together. "You guys were talking about the Blackwell ranch in there, weren't you? Mrs.

Blackwell is the stubborn one you two are trying to pressure. Isn't she?"

"Why are you taking this so personally? This is business. We are being offered an opportunity to be part of something big. We'd be fools not to get in on this when we have the chance."

"At what cost? Running everyone you know out of their homes? Brock, you have a beautiful home. You're fine with that becoming the bottom of a lake?"

Brock put his hands on his hips. "Listen, I was like you. I thought they were going to build their resort here. I didn't realize they were moving up the mountain. It is what it is, though. I don't want to miss out. Mountain Ridge sounds like a dream for your mom. Don't you want your mom to be happy?"

Harper was not going to be emotionally blackmailed. "I'm going to tell my mother and the Blackwells what you're up to. I will make sure that if Mountain Ridge is built, it will be lakeless." She started for the car she had borrowed from her mom.

Brock stopped her again. "What are you doing? You can't ruin this for me. If you ruin this for me, your mother will never forgive

you. I will also make sure that the Blackwells will want nothing to do with you as
well."

"Are you threatening me?"

"I am trying to do what is best for me and
my wife. Your mom hasn't been happy. This
new project will make her feel like she made
the right decision coming here to live with
me. I'm going to ask you again, don't you
want your mom to be happy?"

She turned and walked away without re-
sponding. Of course she wanted her mother
to be happy. That could be true as well as not
wanting to see this town destroyed.

"Think about what you're doing, Harper.
Think about the secrets you're trying to
keep."

That was definitely a threat. Her first
thought was she needed to tell Serena what
was happening and convince her to go back
to Los Angeles with her. Brock wasn't the
person she had thought he was. Not only
was he trying to blackmail her to keep quiet
about all this, what had he done so far to
help make this project a reality? Was he the
reason the loan on the Blackwell ranch had

been called in? Was there any other logical explanation? Didn't seem like it.

Harper started the car but didn't put it in Drive. She thought about how Serena would respond. Who would she choose? History told her that it was unlikely to be her. Serena was too scared to be alone. Her husband had a chance to be one of the first people in on a luxury community. There was little Harper's mom wouldn't love about that.

Brock's threat to reveal her secrets kept her from driving straight to Wyatt and telling him what was happening even though they were the only ones who had the best chance at stopping this. Would he even listen to what she had to say? Wyatt's grandmother figured out she was related to Brock and most likely assumed the worst. Harper couldn't even blame her for thinking that. She had been trying to work with the bad guy even though she didn't know he was the bad guy.

That had to count for something, didn't it?

Maybe leaving town was the best idea. Let these people figure this out themselves. It wasn't like she had anything to gain or lose in this situation. A relationship with

Wyatt was a fantasy that couldn't be a reality no matter how much she thought she wanted it to be. Once again, it had become clear that they were from different worlds that should never have collided.

The old man who had been sitting at the counter came strolling out of the diner. He walked right past Harper and waved. That was when she realized where she had seen him before. At the Flying Spur. That man was Wyatt's great-uncle.

CHAPTER SEVENTEEN

WYATT COULDN'T BELIEVE THAT Harper was nothing but a total manipulator. There was no way he could have fallen that hard for someone who was acting. His raging anxiety wasn't helping him focus on those assertions however.

Harper was masterful at creating a false narrative. She did it on her social media every day. At least, since she had arrived in Eagle Springs. She had the world convinced they were a happily married couple. It was unlikely anyone doubted that was true given the perfect images she posted.

Was he no different than her millions of followers? Duped into believing she was something she was not. Wyatt stopped and doubled over, putting his hands on his knees. It was hard to breathe. There was a weight on his chest that prevented him from taking in the air he needed.

Maybe he had been played for a fool.

He had to harden his heart. If she was a phony, better he figured it out now before he did something he'd truly regret. This marriage would be annulled. He would come clean with his family. He would do everything in his power to help his siblings save this ranch.

Wyatt stood up straight and pushed away his anxiety. He reminded himself that he was better off without any attachments other than his family. He arrived at his trailer only to find Big E standing outside the door.

"You all right?" he asked.

Wyatt readjusted his hat on his head and rolled his shoulder. "I'm fine. What's up?"

"I need to talk to you."

That was the theme of the day. "What's going on?"

"You sent me out to get you some information and I got it. I just don't think you're going to like it."

Wyatt rubbed his eyes and sighed in defeat. Of course he wasn't going to like it. "Tell me."

"I went to the diner for breakfast this morning and your girlfriend was there."

"Did you talk to her?" He really hoped Big E had not talked to her.

"I did not. Mostly because she wasn't alone. Well, she was alone but not for long enough so as I could get to her."

"Let me guess—she was with Brock."

"He showed up eventually, but she was there with the man who showed up here last night to get my sister to sell."

"Mr. Howard? What was she doing with him? Did it seem like she knew who he was? Were they friendly?"

Big E scratched the back of his neck. "She seemed pretty happy to see him when he arrived. They weren't sitting close enough for me to hear what they were talking about, though. Then the banker walked in and sat down with them. The conversation continued; Harper didn't look too pleased with what was being said, and the next thing I knew, she was rushing out of there with Brock hot on her heels."

Wyatt didn't know what to make of that last part. The rest of it told him what he feared—they were all in this together, plotting to take this ranch away from Gran.

"Now, I went to pay my bill while Harper

and Brock had a little conversation outside. When Brock came back in, I heard him tell the guy everything was fine. He made excuses for why she had to leave and promised she would bring her expertise to 'the project.' I didn't catch what the project was, but both of them seemed very pleased with themselves when I left."

Wyatt took off his hat and threw it at Betty. It fell to the ground. "Okay, at least I know."

"We need to talk to Delaney. I don't think we should keep her out of the loop. Clearly, they need this land for something. Maybe they want to build something here. I don't know, but we have to let her know that Brock and this Howard guy are working together. She should be told that Harper is involved."

He was right, but that didn't mean Wyatt wanted to do it. Facing his grandmother and admitting to being a fool was humiliating. He walked over and snatched his hat off the ground. "Let me do it on my own. Your presence always raises her blood pressure. I need her as calm as I can get her."

DENNY WAS IN the house, resting this morning. Her eyes were closed as she sat in her chair in the family room. She was easily wiped out these days.

Wyatt crept into the room with his hat in his hand. The floorboard under his feet creaked and she opened her eyes.

"You done with separating the calves already?"

"We are. The smaller herd is pretty easy to move."

"Next year this time, we'll be back to our usual numbers."

"Let's hope so." Wyatt took a seat on the couch next to her. "I need to talk to you about something."

"Can't be good." She repositioned herself to get a better look at him. "Spill it."

"I messed up, Gran."

"I thought we established that last night," she replied with eyebrows raised.

Wyatt took a deep breath and gathered up the courage to tell the whole truth. "I met Harper in Vegas, but there's more to the story. The reason she followed me to Eagle Springs was because we accidentally got married while we were there."

Gran tipped her head to the side. "Exactly how does one accidentally get married?"

"You have too much to drink and don't remember doing it."

She pinched the bridge of her nose. "Goodness gracious, young man. Nothing good has ever come out of a place where gambling is legal."

He couldn't argue with that right now. "That's why we were sneaking around. I didn't want you to know that I messed up like that."

"Were you two planning to make this work? You know there are things called divorces. Ask your brothers about them—they aren't that hard to get."

"We're going to annul the marriage. Neither one of us realized what we were doing when we signed the papers and said I do. But because of Harper's job, we had to pretend that we were on our honeymoon. That's why we've been hanging out."

"What kind of job requires her to be married to a guy she met in Vegas?"

"I don't know how to begin to explain the internet to you, so you're just going to have to trust me. Playing the part was important for her job."

Gran waved off the need for an explanation. "Okay, so she needed to look happily married. Or at least that's what she told you."

"That was what she told me. She also told me she was thinking about staying in Eagle Springs because she had this opportunity to help the town, but she couldn't give me any specifics. She was very excited about the opportunity, though." Wyatt hung his head in shame. "This is where I really messed up. I let my guard down and I told her things about myself and our family. What I didn't realize was that this opportunity she had was working with Brock and that Mr. Howard you were talking to last night."

Gran inhaled sharply. "I knew it," she mumbled under her breath.

"Big E saw her, Brock and that outsider meeting today to talk about some project they're working on. I can only figure it has something to do with the Flying Spur. I didn't know she was working with them to take your land, Gran. I never would have—"

"Of course you wouldn't have. I never thought you were doing this knowingly. I was mad last night because I figured you weren't making decisions with that brain of yours. You were distracted by her pretty face."

He couldn't argue with that either. "I'm not going to let them take the ranch. I'm here to stay and to help until we get the money. We will get the money."

Gran reached out and gave his hand a squeeze. "I'm sorry your heart got bruised in this fight."

"I wasn't in love with her or anything. I—"

"Don't lie to me or yourself. You're a terrible liar. If you ever go back to Vegas, stay away from the poker tables. You have no poker face."

Wyatt rolled his eyes. "I was falling in love with someone I thought she was. But that's not a real person. It stinks, but I'll survive." It was going to hurt for a while, but he would get over it eventually. He had to believe that.

"Well, now we know that Brock and Xavier Howard are working together to take my ranch. They can try bullying me and messing with my grandkids, but that is not going to deter us from our mission. Once we pay off the loan, they can't touch us. It would be nice to know what they were planning to do with this place. Probably something ridiculous like one of those wellness resorts where they send celebrities who have been in the news too much."

Wyatt realized that maybe he could turn the tables on Brock and be the one getting the information instead of giving it. "I can find out what they're up to. Harper owes me that much. I can go talk to her, sign the annulment papers and get the truth out of her once and for all."

Gran gave his hand one more pat. "Guard that heart."

"I will." He'd try at least.

CHAPTER EIGHTEEN

THE CONVERSATION WITH SERENA went exactly how Harper thought it would go. She defended Brock and his choices. She struggled to understand what was so bad about creating a new community of rich and entitled people. She didn't get why Harper cared what happened to the people of Eagle Springs when they had to give up their homes and businesses just so those rich and entitled residents and visitors of Mountain Ridge could have a lake to look at.

The thing that hurt the most was that she didn't realize that Harper being a part of that plan meant that she would be hurting the man that she loved. Somehow she had fallen in love with Wyatt Blackwell against her better judgment.

"Knock, knock." Serena pushed open Harper's bedroom door. "Is it safe to come in yet? What are you doing?" she asked as soon as she realized Harper was packing.

"I can't stay here, Mom."

Serena started taking things out of the suitcase. "Yes, you can."

Harper tried to take the stack of clothes out of her mom's hands. "Mom, I can't. What Brock is doing is wrong. He's helping this developer run the Blackwells out of town for his own personal benefit. I can't be a part of that. I can't stay under his roof while he's doing that."

"Where are you going to go? There aren't any real hotels in this town. There's one place and it's called the Barn Door Inn. Who would want to stay in a place that has barn in its name?"

Harper took the clothes from Serena and put them back in the suitcase. "This isn't up for debate. I'm leaving."

"You said you wanted me to be happy. You were telling me all of your ideas and I think that if you helped bring those things to life, I would be happy here. Why does it matter if that's here in Eagle Springs or a few miles away in Mountain Ridge?"

Harper sat on the bed and closed her suitcase. "I understand that losing this town wouldn't matter to you, but it matters to some of the other people who live here. It matters to the Blackwells and the Blackwells matter to me."

"They matter more than I do?"

Harper shook her head. "It's not a competition, Mom. They can matter and you can matter at the same time. They also shouldn't have to lose their home and their business so you can have pretty things to look at and upscale cuisine to eat."

"This isn't about those things. It's about Brock. He's my husband, Harper. I am trying to make this marriage work. How can it work if I don't support him when all he's doing is trying to improve our lives?"

"I get it, Mom. I know you want to be a good wife and he thinks that by doing this he's being a good husband. The ends don't justify the means, though. What he's doing is wrong. And I think a good wife tells her husband when he's doing something that's wrong."

"Are you sure you've really looked at all the costs and benefits of this plan? Maybe the Blackwells would—"

"Mom, stop," Harper interrupted. "I can't do this with you anymore. I love you. I hope that you and Brock have a great life together. You aren't wrong about me wanting you to be happy here."

"I'm happiest when you're close by." Serena's eyes were wet. "When I can spend time with you. I don't want you to leave."

Harper gave her mom a hug. How did all of this go so wrong so fast? Yesterday, Harper was thinking about staying in Eagle Springs for as long as Wyatt was going to be here. She believed she was going to be part of a revitalization project that would attract people to Eagle Springs, not swim in it. Now she had to figure out how to say goodbye to all of it.

The doorbell rang and Serena pulled back. "Who could that be?"

Harper offered to go check. The handsome cowboy she'd been falling in love with stood on the other side of the door. His jeans were dirty and his eyes were sad.

"We need to talk," he said. His tone was less than friendly and it caused the muscles in her shoulders to tense.

"Sure, come on in." She swung the door open and moved aside so he could enter.

"Can you come out here? I don't feel comfortable stepping foot inside Brock's home."

Harper didn't blame him for feeling that way. Brock was doing everything in his power to do Wyatt's family wrong. She stepped out onto the porch and closed the door behind her. There was a bench out there, so she motioned for him to sit.

"I have a lot to tell you," she said.

His expression stayed grim. "I sure hope so because I have a lot of questions."

"Questions?"

"Has this all been some sort of game to you? I know when we met in Vegas there was no way you could have known I was going to be in that casino at that time. That part of all this had to be a coincidence, but at some point I became your mark and I can't figure out when that was."

"My mark?"

"Isn't that what they call the person you're trying to swindle?"

Harper felt confused and hurt by that accusation. "You think I have been trying to swindle you?"

"Isn't that what this has been? You spend time with me, putting me at ease until I tell you things that you can pass on to Brock who passes them on to Mr. Howard?"

"Xavier Howard? How do you know Xavier? And what information was passed on to him?" Harper thought back to the conversation Brock and Xavier were having at the diner that made no sense. The one that was clearly about Wyatt's grandmother. Xavier had said something about insider information.

"Mr. Howard, I don't know if his first name is Xavier, we weren't really on a first-name basis when he came over yesterday to coerce my grandmother into selling our ranch. It was pretty unbelievable that you would tell them to use her illness against her."

Harper sat down; she felt dizzy. "He used her illness to coerce your grandmother into selling the ranch? Wyatt, you have to believe me, that was never my intention. I don't remember telling Brock she was sick." She replayed all their recent conversations. The stress of it made her doubt if she could remember correctly. "Maybe I did. I honestly don't remember. It certainly wasn't a conversation about how to get your grandma to sell the ranch. I have never had that conversation."

Wyatt paced in front of her. "That's really hard to believe when I know you met with the guy this morning to talk about his new project. I also had a visit from Brock today who let me know that you've told him everything like how we got married in Vegas. He also made it clear that if I didn't try to convince my gran to sell, he'd be sure she disowned me for lying to her."

Harper's head fell into her hands. She had betrayed Wyatt's trust by giving hers to Brock. "I can't believe he did that. I'm sorry. I never should have told him. I thought that I was doing something good and it turns out I was working for the wrong side."

"I want to believe you. I thought you and I were feeling the same things. I feel like a complete fool, but I can't fall for any more lies."

Harper's head snapped up. "I never lied to you. Well, maybe I lied by omission, but I never straight-up lied. I was… I *am* feeling the same things. I didn't realize how deep

Brock was into this and neither one of us knew Xavier's real plan. We were all sort of duped."

Wyatt sat down next to her on the bench. "What is Xavier's real plan?"

"I thought he wanted to help revitalize Eagle Springs and build on to it. I thought I was going to be a part of shining things up and attracting new businesses to town."

"He had plans for more than just the Flying Spur? Please tell me what is going on," Wyatt pleaded.

Harper's shoulders sank. She hated that she had almost had a part in what Xavier had planned for Eagle Springs. "It's not just your ranch they're after, but you have to lose your ranch for everything else to fall into place."

"They want other properties?"

"I need you to believe me when I say I did not know until today what the grand plan was. I know your great-uncle was at the diner. I saw him. I know he saw me with Xavier and Brock. I'm sure he thinks the worst of me, but I sure hope he told you that I left that meeting. I walked out because I do not want to be associated with what they want to do."

Wyatt stared down at his hand in his lap. "He did say you looked upset and left. But he said Brock followed you out and when he came back inside, he assured the other guy that everything was fine and you were on board."

Brock needed her to get his piece of Mountain Ridge. Xavier saw her as the bigger asset moving forward. It was no wonder he told Xavier she was still interested. He probably thought he could convince her to reconsider.

"He lied. I know you're having trouble believing me, but I did not tell Brock I was on board with any of this. I came back here, talked to my mom and started packing my bags. I can't stay here under the same roof as someone who would turn his back on his entire town."

"What's that mean? Are they going to knock down the whole town and put up condos or something?" Wyatt turned those hazel eyes on her. She had fallen in love with his eyes the minute she met him. They were kind and curious. She absolutely loved that about him. Her heart was breaking, knowing he didn't think she deserved his kindness anymore.

"Worse. They want to make the valley a lake. The only place they want to build something is north of here in a place they call Mountain Ridge."

She could see on his face that he was just as confused as Brock was when Xavier had said the name. "Mountain Ridge?"

"That's what they're going to call it. It doesn't exist yet. They have plans to make it a mountain resort town like Breckenridge or Aspen."

Wyatt was back on his feet. He didn't hide his disgust. His tone was full of it. "Somewhere the people of Eagle Springs could never afford to live. They think they're just going to take it all?"

"It's terrible. I don't want that for the people of Eagle Springs. I've fallen in love with this town. I hope you believe me."

"It doesn't matter. My focus needs to be on my family right now. I've been distracted long enough."

"Is that what I was? Just a distraction?"

Wyatt's discomfort in talking about them

was obvious. "We need to sign those papers, Harper. We need to annul the marriage as soon as possible. Our deal is done."

Harper knew it was coming, but hearing him say it still stung. "I know. I emailed my lawyer this morning, asking her to draw them up."

"I'm sorry this is bad for your business. I just can't pretend anymore."

Had that been all they were doing? Pretending to feel something for one another? Not Harper. Her feelings were authentic. The marriage was an accident but their connection felt very real. "I have so many pictures from this weekend, I should be able to make those stretch the rest of the week. I'll bring over the papers as soon as I get them."

"Good. Thank you." He started for the steps but turned back. "Where are you planning to stay if you're leaving here?"

"My mom said there's a place called the Barn Door Inn. I was thinking about going there. I did an internet search and there's also a hotel called Finley's. I might check that out."

"No, you don't want to stay at Finley's. That's where ranch hands and rodeo competitors stay. That's not for out of town guests like you. The Barn Door is a better choice. If that doesn't work out, call me. I'll find a room for you somewhere."

Harper wanted to cry. He still thought she was worthy of his kindness. "Thank you. I really appreciate that."

"I want to believe that you are who I thought you were."

"I am. I am so sorry that Brock used our secret against you and that he took things I told him and shared them with Xavier. Your grandmother must think I am a terrible person."

"She is only focused on keeping people from taking her ranch away. Once you go back to California, she won't think about you at all."

Another dagger right to the heart. Once she left Wyoming, would he not think about her either? She was afraid that the memories she'd made over the last couple weeks would be with her forever but tainted by how things ended unfortunately.

"Please tell her that I am sorry for my part in causing her any trouble. I know I don't matter, but I want her to understand that I had no intention of doing any harm to your family."

Wyatt's jaw was tense. He swallowed hard and then cleared his throat. "I'll tell her. Goodbye, Harper."

He took off without as much as a glance back. She wouldn't see him again until she handed him the papers to annul their marriage. The tears began to run down her face. This wasn't how she wanted this to end.

"How did that go?" her mom poked her head out the front door. Harper wiped her cheeks, and Serena took notice. "That bad, huh? I'm sorry, honey."

Not sorry enough to tell Brock he was wrong. Not sorry enough to help do the right thing. Harper took a deep breath and wiped her face one more time. "It's fine. We weren't going to end up together. We were always going to go our own ways. I don't know why I'm letting it hurt this much."

"Maybe I can ask Brock to talk to him and explain that you didn't want to be part of Mountain Ridge. If he's the one, you shouldn't let him g—"

Harper's frustration overflowed. "Brock already talked to Wyatt, Mom. He's been talking to a lot of people apparently. Did you know that he was telling Xavier things I told him? Or that he went to the Blackwells' today to threaten Wyatt with exposing our marriage to his family if he didn't try to convince his grandmother to sell her ranch?"

"Honey, Brock wouldn't—"

"Don't say he wouldn't because you don't know him any better than I do. You want to know the really sad part? I was actually starting to like Brock. For the first time in forever, I thought you had married a nice guy, someone I could get along with and wouldn't mind spending time with when I visited you. But he's been using me to get this deal with Xavier and to hurt the Blackwells. I don't know how to process that right now."

Harper stood up. She didn't want to hear her mom defend Brock for doing the indefensible. She went in the house to get her suitcase and call a cab.

CHAPTER NINETEEN

IT WAS QUITE POSSIBLE that the Blackwell dinner table had never been as quiet as it was that Monday evening. Wyatt was at the same time glad for it and a bit unnerved. Even the children seemed to know that tonight was not the night to be chatty. Big E was notably missing. Gran picked at her food. Wyatt couldn't tell if it was because her treatment earlier in the day had taken some of her appetite or if it was because she was too distracted by the latest drama.

Nash swallowed down his water so loudly, Wyatt wondered if he was hiding a microphone and speaker somewhere to amplify the sound of it. Mason, who was sitting next to Nash, made eye contact with Wyatt across the table as if to acknowledge that was as weird and annoying as Wyatt thought it was.

"The chicken was seasoned perfectly, Mason," Ryder said, unable to stay silent any longer. He had spent the whole meal glancing anxiously at each of the Blackwells.

"It was delicious," Corliss added.

"Thanks, I added a little bit of paprika this time. I think it was a nice change from the chili powder that I usually use."

When Wyatt was fourteen, the only powder he used to cook with came from inside a box of mac and cheese.

"When you open your own restaurant someday, will we have to come there every night for dinner or will you come home to cook for us?" Nash asked.

"I think one of us might need to learn how to cook," Corliss said. "Not it."

"Don't look at me." Nash tossed his napkin on his plate. "If you put me in charge, we're only eating ham-and-swiss sandwiches for the rest of our lives."

"Maybe Mason can teach me how to cook," little Olivia offered.

"That's very sweet of you, honey," Ryder said. "But it should be one of the grown-ups. At some point, we're going to have to fend for ourselves."

"True," Nash said.

"Give a man a fish and he'll be hungry

in an hour, teach him how to fish and you feed him for a lifetime. Isn't that the saying?" Ryder asked.

"It makes no sense, though," Nash said after thinking about it for a second. "I can catch fish all day but have no idea how to cook it."

Mason shook his head and chuckled. "You guys are going to be in big trouble when I go to college."

When dinner was over, Corliss asked Wyatt to help clean up. Ryder offered to take the kids for some ice cream in town. That was clearly planned. Before they left, Adele and the twins walked in. Ryder took all four kids to Tucker's. The man was a saint.

"When is Levi getting here?" Wyatt asked as he dried one of the drinking glasses Corliss had set on the drying rack.

"Should be any minute."

"Guess we're having a family meeting to discuss what an idiot I am and how I almost single-handedly lost the ranch for us?"

Corliss huffed and rolled her eyes. "Wow, you sure are giving yourself a lot of credit, aren't you?"

"Turned out, I was sleeping with the

enemy just like you accused me of. I told her things in confidence and she let them slip to Brock. Who knows what else she told him that he hasn't used against us yet? What if he meddles in our attempts to raise the money? He could still make trouble for us."

"That's why we're having a family meeting. We need to talk about how to handle Brock and this Xavier Howard guy. We aren't going to dwell on what happened between you and Harper."

Wyatt had a hard time believing none of his siblings were going to give him a hard time. It was amazing that Nash had held his tongue since he found out what happened.

Levi came waltzing in a few minutes later. "Sorry I'm late. I had to stop by Brock's and hand over my detailed plan for how I was going to get my twenty grand to pay off the loan so he could mess with it."

That didn't take long.

"Ha, ha. Didn't you read my text?" Corliss asked, flicking some suds at him.

"What? The one that said don't be mean to poor, baby Wyatt, he's really upset? Yeah, I read it."

Wyatt refused to jump at the bait. He took

a deep breath and blew it out slowly. They had every right to be mad at him and to give him flack. Corliss didn't need to protect him from it.

"Real nice, Levi. Let's hope you never make any mistakes in your life or fall for the wrong person."

"You weren't really serious about this woman, were you? You've known her for like three weeks. How could you have fallen for her already?"

Wyatt wanted to laugh it off and be very clear that he had no feelings for Harper. Levi was right; they barely knew each other. It would be ridiculous to think he could have been in love with her. But the pain in his chest stopped him. Why did it hurt like he was in love with her?

Corliss had lost her patience. "Can you go wait for us in the family room?" Levi didn't argue. He left them to finish the dishes. "I'm sorry about that."

"You didn't need to tell them to be nice to me."

She handed him the last plate to dry. "I did because I can tell you're hurting, little brother."

He shrugged but didn't deny it. She gave him a side hug.

"Thanks," he managed to squeak out even though his throat was tight with emotion.

They finished the dishes and went out to join the others for the family meeting. Wyatt was ready to face the music. It was unlikely that Levi was the only one who was going to ignore Corliss's request to be kind.

"Okay, so we just want to get everyone on the same page. Wyatt found out today that there is a developer looking to take over our land and then the rest of Eagle Springs, but he's not looking to build here. He wants to put the valley underwater."

Adele's attention was fully captured. "Wait, what?"

"Once they get our land, they think everyone else will fold. We don't have all the details, but we know their endgame is a luxury resort town in the mountains that will look down on this valley, which they would like to turn into a lake."

"Whoa, your girlfriend doesn't want to just take our ranch, she wants to take the whole town, huh?" Levi chimed in.

"She doesn't want to do anything. She

thought they were going to revitalize the town. As soon as she found out their real intentions, she backed out. And she's not my girlfriend."

"She's his wife," Gran shared.

Wyatt was waiting for that little tidbit to get out. He didn't expect it to come from his grandmother.

"She's what?" Levi exclaimed, bug-eyed.

"Neither one of us remembers it, but apparently we got married in Vegas. We're annulling it as soon as her lawyer draws up the papers."

Levi looked to Nash. "Did you know about this?"

Nash played innocent. "I only found out today, but Corliss forced me not to say anything until we had the family meeting."

"Can we stay focused here? What's going on has nothing to do with Wyatt or his… or Harper," she said, opting not to label her. "It has nothing to do with Harper. In fact, we should be happy that she clued us in. She may have accidentally told Brock a few things about us, but she told us everything she knows about this project to destroy Eagle Springs."

Wyatt had never wanted to hug his sister as much as he did right then. He managed to give her a small smile when she glanced in his direction instead.

"I think it's obvious that we need to hold Brock in the center of town and make him explain to everyone in Eagle Springs why he wants to take their homes and businesses away," Nash suggested.

Gran shook her head. "Brock has no power. He is doing everything he can to get in on this deal with Xavier, but he can't take our ranch if we pay off the loan."

"That's where our focus needs to stay," Corliss said. "We all must stick to the plan. If we come up with the money, there is no way they can take the Flying Spur and without the Flying Spur, no one else will sell to them."

"But keep your eyes and ears open," Gran warned. "Who knows who else might be in on this deal and be willing to help Xavier spoil our plans."

Wyatt's phone rang and all eyes were on him. Everyone who would call him was sitting in the room, which meant it could only be one person. He excused himself to answer it.

"Hello."

"Hey, Wyatt, I'm sorry to bother you. I just wanted you to know that I have the annulment papers. I had to go to three places to find someone with a printer, but I got them. If you want, we can meet tomorrow."

"Tonight. I can come tonight. You're at the Barn Door Inn?"

"Room 2." Her voice was small. Sad.

Wyatt felt that same overwhelming sadness, but this needed to be done. The sooner he signed those papers, the sooner he could get back to his real life. He hung up and went into the family room.

"Who was that?" Adele asked.

"I'll give you one guess," Levi said.

"I'm going to go sign my annulment papers so this part of the nightmare can be over."

THE BARN DOOR INN probably wasn't like the other hotels Harper stayed in when she went on vacation. Wyatt never understood why they named it the way they did. It didn't look like a barn or have a barn door. It had actually been the general store back when Gran first came to town. In the 1980s, the two-story building was renovated into a hotel. It wasn't glamorous, but it was for the more typical guests of Eagle Ridge, unlike Finley's, which was for traveling cowboys.

Wyatt stood outside Harper's room for a couple minutes before knocking. This would most likely be the last time he was ever going to see Harper and knowing that made it difficult to proceed. Saying goodbye was something Wyatt did all the time. He traveled from city to city, state to state. He met people, spent a couple months with them, then moved on like it was nothing. Moving on from Harper was far from nothing.

He knocked and she answered the door with eyes that were red and swollen from crying. Wyatt immediately felt protective.

"Are you okay?" he asked, looking past her to see if someone else was there making her upset.

"I'm fine. It's been a tough day. I've been feeling a little sorry for myself. That's all. Come on in." She opened the door wide and stepped aside so he could enter.

The urge to hold her in his arms and tell

her everything would be okay was strong, but he resisted. Harper skipped all the small talk and went straight to the small desk in the corner and picked up a pen. "I already signed. Once you sign, it's done."

Done. One scribble and it would be done. Wyatt's feet felt cemented to the floor. He had come there to be done with this. Why was it the last thing he wanted at the moment?

"How long are you planning on staying here?" he asked, delaying the inevitable.

"I'm trying to find a flight out as soon as possible so hopefully no more than a couple nights. I figured I can hide here and stay out of trouble."

Last night, Wyatt had tossed the list of things he planned to do with her these next couple weeks in the garbage. This morning, he had pulled that list out. Harper had opened his heart back up to this town, and with the threat of losing everything in town hanging over his head, he wanted to appreciate everything Eagle Springs had to offer. Even if he had to do it without Harper.

"Maybe you can get over to Tucker's one more time for ice cream before you go. I'm sure he'd like to see his favorite customer one more time."

Harper let out a small laugh but the smile didn't stick. "I don't feel like anyone's favorite anything at the moment."

Guilt had been niggling at him since they had cleared the air. He didn't want her to feel this way. The more he thought about it, the more he realized that it was his fault she was caught up in this drama, not hers. Had she not met him, she never would have been dragged into this.

"I believe you didn't know what you were getting yourself into. I don't think you were trying to steal my family's ranch away. I think you should know that before you go. I don't want you to leave under the impression that there's bad blood between us."

Harper pressed her lips together and her eyes welled with fresh tears. She nodded but chose not to speak as she tried to gather her composure.

"I had more fun the last couple weeks than I have had in my whole life here in Eagle Springs. You made me like being home and if you knew me well, you'd know that was a very big deal."

The tears flowed freely and she grabbed a tissue from the box on the nightstand by her bed. He noticed that she had his painting sitting on the dresser. That had been such a fun night. Every time he was with Harper, it was fun.

"You don't have to be nice to me," she said with a sob.

He willed his feet to move and go to her. He wrapped her up in his arms and she cried even harder. "I may not have to—I want to," he said, meaning every word.

"Hurting you is a regret I will carry with me for the rest of my life. You have been nothing but kind and patient with me. You were willing to help me even though my ask was awful big. All I wanted was to have more reasons to stay and be close to you and instead, I ruined everything."

Wyatt held her a little tighter as she cried. She had been so excited the other day when she told him about this opportunity she had to make Eagle Springs better. She really had thought that Brock and Xavier were giving her a chance to do something positive for this town.

"Tonight at my family meeting, my sister

had your back. She made it clear to everyone else that if it wasn't for you, we wouldn't know what kind of no-good these types were up to. You are not the bad guy in this story, Harper."

"Thank you for saying that."

He pulled back just far enough to see her face. "I mean it."

She touched his cheek and looked up at him like she was trying to memorize everything about his face. "I really enjoyed being your wife, Cowboy Wyatt."

Now she was getting him choked up. He brushed the back of his hand against her cheek. Goodbye wasn't going to be hard. It was going to be impossible. He lowered his face to hers. One kiss wouldn't cause too much trouble.

A loud pounding on the door caused Harper to jump. She opened the door only to find her mom, the man from the front desk and about seven suitcases.

"I did it, Harper. I left him. I left Brock."

CHAPTER TWENTY

Spacious was not how anyone would describe the room at the Barn Door Inn. It felt even smaller with Wyatt, Harper's mother and her mother's seven suitcases sharing the space.

Harper sat on the bed since there was little room for all of them to stand. "I wasn't expecting you to pack up and leave," she said to her mom, still stunned by her arrival.

Serena moved her bags around, organizing them from largest to smallest. "I didn't know what else to do. I told him that he should try to get his friend to build his resort here in Eagle Springs instead of making it a lake. I told him he should listen to you and your ideas."

She was quiet for a second, seemingly lost in her thoughts.

"And?"

Snapping out of it, she replied, "He went

off about how I didn't understand and that I shouldn't tell him how to do business. He said that he was doing all this for me, but I don't want him to do this for me if it means that my daughter can't stand to be in the same house as us." Serena fought back the tears. "You're more important than anything else."

Her mom had chosen her. Harper couldn't help but feel a bit smug about that. At the same time, she didn't believe Brock would give up without a fight.

"He just watched you leave?" Harper asked, needing more context.

"Not exactly. He went to get dinner, thinking that I needed to eat something to see things clearly. I packed up some of my stuff and left."

This was only some of her stuff? Brock was going to freak out when he got home and found *some* of her things missing. She shifted her gaze to Wyatt, who was stuck in the back corner of the room by the desk. The desk with their annulment papers sitting there waiting for his signature.

"I have a feeling he's going to be blowing up your phone very soon if he hasn't already."

"I'm sorry for barging in here and taking over. I'm happy to see that you two are on better terms," Serena said, grinning at Wyatt.

Wyatt climbed over Serena's bags. "You two can't stay in this tiny room together. Let me help you find somewhere else to stay."

"You don't have to do that," Harper said at the same time as Serena thanked him profusely. "Mom, we can both spend the night here and figure out what to do next tomorrow morning. Wyatt does not need to rehome us."

"It's not a big deal. We can check to see if the hotel has another room available and if not, you could have your mom stay here and you can crash in Betty. I can sleep on the couch in my gran's house."

"You are not going to sleep on the couch because my mother brought every piece of clothing in her wardrobe to my hotel room."

Wyatt's half grin caused Harper to smile for the first time today. He was definitely about to kiss her before Serena showed up.

She really hoped they'd get the chance to finish what he started before she left town.

"I'm happy to help you out. Wouldn't you do the same thing if the tables were turned?"

"You know I would," she replied with certainty.

"I'll go downstairs and ask about another room," he offered.

Serena joined Harper on the bed and lay back on the pillows. "Can you see if they have a room with a queen-size bed? I don't think I can sleep on a full."

"Queen bed, got it." Wyatt gave them a salute. He opened the door and ran right into Brock.

"What are you doing here?" Brock asked, taking a step back.

Harper flew off the bed and pulled Wyatt away from the man he probably wanted to punch more than anyone in Eagle Springs. "What are *you* doing here?" she asked Brock.

The man looked like she felt earlier. "I'm here to talk to my wife. I'm here to beg her to come home. Serena, please."

"You need to go home, Brock," Serena

said from the bed. "I don't want to talk to you."

Brock's words were dripping in clear desperation. "Please, baby. I know you're mad. I am sorry for being such a jerk. It's hard for me to admit that I made a mistake, so I shouted and said some very hurtful things to you. I shouldn't have done that."

"No, you shouldn't have," Serena replied.

"You have to believe me. Everything I've done, I've done for you. If you don't want me to do anything else, I won't do anything else. I can't change what's happened, but I can stay out of it moving forward."

"You would do that?" Harper asked. "You would let Xavier know you don't support destroying Eagle Springs?"

"I can let him know you and I aren't interested in working on the Mountain Ridge project. Please, Harper, all I want to do is to be a good husband. I thought that if I got in on this deal that your mother would see me as a real success. She came out here to Wyoming because she thought I was somebody important. When she got here, I started to fear she was disappointed I wasn't as important as I led her to believe."

Serena got off the bed and came to the door. "You thought I was disappointed in who you are?"

"My family has lived in Eagle Springs for generations. We're small-town folk. You come from a big city. You're used to having whatever you need at your fingertips and being surrounded by pretty things. I worried you didn't find enough pretty things around here. Until Harper got here, you seemed depressed."

Harper had noticed the same. Serena needed Harper to show her how to appreciate what this town had to offer. Otherwise, her mom's marriage to Brock was going to end just like Harper predicted when they got together.

Brock held Serena's hands in his. "Xavier misled me so I'd believe that I was going to help him make Eagle Springs somewhere you'd want to live."

Harper couldn't help but steal a glance in Wyatt's direction. They weren't that different from Serena and Brock. Two people from different worlds trying to figure it out. Did Wyatt ever wonder if she'd be happy settling down somewhere like this with him?

"Oh, Brock." Serena was swooning. She wrapped her arms around his neck, hugging him tight. "Why did you wait until I packed all my stuff up to tell me this?"

"I'm a stubborn fool and I didn't think you'd leave."

"Can you reinstate my grandmother's loan?" Wyatt asked, unimpressed by their reconciliation.

Serena let Brock go. "You can do that, right, honey?"

"I can't, Wyatt. The note has been called in and there's no way the bank is going to give her another loan while that one is outstanding. I didn't think Denny would hold out the way she has, but she's more stubborn than I am. If you guys can pay back the loan, I'm sure the bank would be willing to extend some credit again."

"That doesn't help them save their ranch from being taken away right now," Harper reminded him.

"I know, and I'd say I'm sorry, but that doesn't do you any good. I acted selfishly. I helped the wrong people for what I thought was the right reason. I never expected the plan was to wipe Eagle Springs off the map.

I truly believed they were going to make Eagle Springs the premiere vacation destination in Wyoming. I was just as surprised as you were this morning."

Harper had noticed that. There was no way Brock knew what they were really planning. She also believed he had the same intentions she did. They had both wanted to bring some pretty things to Eagle Springs to make her mom happy. It didn't change the fact that he had been completely on board with forcing the Blackwells off their land.

"You're right about one thing. You saying sorry doesn't mean much," Wyatt said, his hands balled into fists. "I should go."

"Wyatt, wait." Harper pointed an angry finger at Brock's chest. "You are going to make this right. If you can't give them their loan back, then you are going to do everything in your power to make sure they are able to pay it off. That means you will not interfere with their plans to pay off the loan. You will support any Blackwell family member's moneymaking venture. It will become your personal mission in life to see that they have everything they need to stay in Eagle Springs. You will not only tell Xavier Howard we aren't interested in Mountain Ridge, you will stand up for Eagle Springs. You will not feed him any information that can help him pressure Wyatt's grandma into selling. You will instead tell us everything you know about him so that the Blackwells have a fighting chance."

Serena stood beside her daughter. "That sounds about right. A man who does all that would be a man I would be proud to call my husband."

"Xavier is a—a—a—a very powerful businessman," Brock sputtered. "I'm not sure that's someone we want to make our enemy, Serena."

"Then I guess Wyatt should go ask about getting me a room here at the inn. I won't go home with someone unwilling to take a stand and protect the town and the people who have made him who he is."

Harper had never been so proud of her mom. She was holding her ground and standing up for what was right. Wyatt started for the door.

"No, stop," Brock insisted. "Fine. I'll do what I can to help. I can't change what's happened, but I can refuse to be part of anything else moving forward. Xavier thought Harper was going to be his ticket to attracting businesses to the area. Without her, he's got to find another way. That should help delay their project a bit."

"That sounds good," Serena said. "If Brock does all that, would you be willing to stay? I don't want you to go yet, Harper. Brock was right about me feeling depressed until you got here. Please reconsider leaving."

Harper's eyes flickered in Wyatt's direction, assessing his reaction to the possibility of her sticking around town. His expression didn't give away how he might feel.

"I'll think about it," she said, wanting to talk to Wyatt before she made her mom any promises. If he didn't want her around, she would have to go. She had caused him enough trouble. "Let's get you and your suitcases downstairs and back to Brock's. You have a lot of unpacking to do."

They each grabbed a couple of Serena's bags and loaded up Brock's car. Serena handed the keys to her car to Harper. "Come home when you can. You are always welcome."

"I think you and Brock deserve a night alone, but I'll check out of here in the morning. I need you to know that I appreciate that you were on my side tonight. It means a lot."

Serena carefully cradled Harper's face in her hands. "You have always been the most important thing in my life, and I am sorry I have not always made you feel that way. I will not make that mistake again."

Serena and Brock went home and left Wyatt and Harper on the sidewalk outside the Barn Door Inn. The street was blanketed in a velvety darkness and peaceful quiet. Everyone was home and settled in for the night.

"Well, that was interesting," Wyatt said with his hands in his back pockets.

"Never a dull moment with Serena. She's full of drama and intrigue."

Wyatt's gaze fell to the ground at his feet. "I should head home. Let the family know that Brock won't be a problem moving forward."

"Yeah, of course. I hope that takes some of the stress off everyone's shoulders. I'm sorry there isn't more he could do. I wish I could just make your debt disappear." A thought popped in her head that seemed like the perfect solution. "Hey, I could start a fund-raiser on my social media. Ask my followers to donate to save the ranch. I'm sure we could raise a ton of money that way."

"Oh no," Wyatt said, looking panicked. "No, no, no. My gran's pride wouldn't stand for it. That would be worse than losing the ranch. We have to do this the right way. We need to earn it."

"It's not a big deal. There are a lot of nice people out there who want to donate to a good cause. Saving your family's ranch, saving this town would be a good cause."

"You've really fallen in love with this place, haven't you?"

Harper had fallen in love with a few things. "I have never felt truly at home until I came here. It has a lot to do with the people who live here, I think."

"Like your mom," he said, stepping closer.

"She's one of them. There's more. Tucker makes me feel very welcome. Even if he tells lots of people they're his favorite customer."

Wyatt barked out a laugh. "Tucker, of course."

"There's Mr. Littlejohn who finds my enthusiasm for astronomy delightful."

Wyatt's smile made his eyes crinkle at the edges. "Yes, you would have been his star student if you had been here in high school."

"Jill and I would have totally been besties if I had lived here when we were in high school. She's very sweet."

"She would have killed to be your friend," Wyatt said, nodding. "I think everyone would have wanted to be friends with you."

"Even you?" As soon as she asked the question, she feared the answer.

Wyatt's expression changed from playful to serious. "I don't think I could have been your friend," he said, sending her hopes crashing down. Still, he stepped closer until they were standing toe-to-toe.

Harper stiffened but forced herself to soften her shoulders. It was embarrassing that she had believed that the two of them could have a relationship. Wyatt might not hate her, but he couldn't imagine them even being friends.

She dropped her gaze. "Right, we're much too different."

Wyatt put his fingers under her chin and encouraged her to look back up at him.

"That's not why I couldn't be your friend. The issue is I would have wanted to be more than friends with you. I would have been head over heels in love with you, and I know that's a fact because it's how I feel right now. I love you, Harper."

Harper's heart nearly leaped from her chest. She wanted to ask him to repeat that one more time, but she didn't want to miss the chance to tell him she felt the same way. "I love you, too."

He brought his face close to hers and she sensed the breath of his words on her lips. "That's a relief. This would have been awfully awkward if you didn't."

He pressed his lips against hers. His hand moved from her chin to the nape of her neck, pulling her closer. Her whole body was trembling. Heat crawled up her cheeks. Harper felt like she was in some kind of fairy tale only instead of a crown, her Prince Charming wore a Stetson.

When the kiss ended, Harper kept her eyes closed to relish the feeling for a moment longer. She had been ready to leave this place for good, and now she never wanted to go.

"I can't believe I didn't stop you and kiss you upstairs in your room. I have never been more attracted to a woman than when you were jabbing Brock in the chest and telling him how it was going to be. I love how strong and fearless you are."

"I don't know about fearless. I felt scared today. Scared that I was never going to feel this way about anyone else. You have ruined me for all other men. My expectations are going to be far too high."

He rewarded her with an amused grin. "I guess you better not try to meet any new guys then."

Her heart sighed happily. A ripple of contentment flowed through her. There would be no other. Cowboy Wyatt was the only one she wanted. Harper found herself back in his arms; she took advantage of being close and kissed him again.

"You want to go upstairs and sign those annulment papers?" she asked when they came up for air.

He ran the pad of his thumb across her bottom lip. His eyes were filled with affection. "Not tonight. I am going to go home and let my family know what's happening.

Plus, I think I want to be married to you a little bit longer."

Harper had no reason to object.

CHAPTER TWENTY-ONE

"Hello to my friends all over the world. I am here livestreaming with my totally gorgeous and amazing husband, Cowboy Wyatt. He has a secret account on here so he can make sure I don't post any unflattering pictures of him." She lowered her voice like she was telling them a secret. "It's impossible to take an unflattering picture of him, by the way."

She thought he was so funny. The last thing he wanted was her followers to try to find him on social media. He'd have to spend the whole night denying follow requests. "Tell them not to follow me. I don't post anything. It would be pointless."

Harper held her phone out so they were both in the frame of the video. Wyatt waved at the screen. Apparently people from all over the world were watching this from the comfort of their homes. Wyatt went back to brushing Kingston, his chocolate-brown quarter horse.

"You heard him, people. Do not follow him. He's boring. You know what's not boring? The ranch life. We are here at the Flying Spur and it's time to go horseback riding."

Wyatt watched as Harper introduced the horses to her followers. She was wearing her new black cowboy hat. They had bought it in town the other day before they met Gina Sullivan and her boyfriend for dinner. The Western style looked good on her. Of course, she could wear anything and look beautiful. He heard her announce that the link to buy their own hat was in the comments. Knowing the effect she had on people, some hat company was about to make a lot of money.

Wyatt set the pad on Kingston's back and put on his saddle. Once that was secure, he made sure the cinch was snug enough on Harper's saddle and then checked the throatlatch to make sure it wouldn't bother the horse.

"Okay, what can I do?" Harper asked, clapping her hands together. He noticed her phone was already tucked into her back pocket.

"You aren't bringing your social media friends along for the ride?"

"Not live," she said as if it should have been obvious. "No one wants to watch a livestream for that long. We'll take pictures and videos while we ride and I'll upload them later."

Wyatt nodded. She always had a plan. "All right. Are you ready to go then?"

"I'm ready," she said in the most unconvincing way. "Actually, I'm terrified but totally ready."

He was completely in love with this woman. She had never been on a horse before. Wyatt had convinced her that it was easier than riding a bike and she'd love it. Then, she watched Olivia learning to ride the other day and the kid took a dive. The little girl was fine. Tough as nails in fact. But now, Harper was sure that any horse she got on was going to buck her off. Yet, here she was prepared to face the challenge head-on.

He put a hand on her shoulder and could feel the tension right away. "Horses are very tuned to your feelings. If it picks up on your fear and anxiety, it's going to get anxious. You need to relax. I am not going to let anything happen to you."

He watched as her trust in him pushed the fear aside. She flashed him one of those smiles that made his heart skip a couple beats. "I know you won't. That's why I'm still going to do this even though I'm scared."

"Where are you two headed?" Corliss stood by the gate outside the paddock where they were preparing for their ride. She held a hand above her eyes to shield them from the sun.

"I'm teaching Harper how to ride," Wyatt answered. "I also want to go check those new fences I put in, make sure the elk are getting over them safely."

"Were you able to fix the clutch on the tractor?" she asked. She was hovering because Harper was here. Corliss was sure that his guest would be a distraction.

"I fixed it before lunch. I've been checking off all the boxes on your list today, sis. Everything will be done by dinnertime."

"He's not going to be here for dinner, though," Harper said, sounding apologetic.

She didn't need to feel bad about him choosing to spend time with her. His family saw him plenty.

"I remember. Gran asked me to remind you that she wants to talk to you before you leave. Both of you."

Wyatt led the horses over to where he wanted Harper to mount. "Yeah, we know."

"Does she seem like she's in a good mood today?" Harper asked. "When she asked you to tell us that she wanted to talk to us was it a pleasant request like, 'I'd really like to talk to Wyatt and Harper before they leave for dinner.' Or was it more gruff? 'Tell Wyatt and Harper to get their butts in here before they leave.'" Harper's impression of Gran was spot-on.

Corliss and Wyatt couldn't help but crack up. Poor Harper had worked hard the last week and a half to get to know everyone in his family, but she was trying the hardest to win over Gran.

"She definitely demanded butts in the house before you leave," Corliss warned.

Harper's face fell.

"That doesn't mean she's upset about anything. That's just the way she talks," Wyatt tried to reassure her.

Harper tried to act like she believed that. "Right. We should go so we can get back. I don't want her to be more mad because we're hustling out of there to be on time for dinner."

"She's not mad. Thanks a lot, Corliss!" he shouted at his sister who had already started walking away. His sister gave him a you're welcome wave.

"Seriously, she likes you. Gran even asked me if you liked apple or peach pie yesterday. I think she's planning on inviting you for dinner this weekend and wants to impress you with a pie from Sweetwater Kitchen downtown. She thinks their pies are the best in all of Wyoming."

Harper's face lit up. "For real?"

"I would not lie about pie."

"What did you tell her?"

"I told her apple," he replied.

"You chose for me? Why didn't you ask me?"

"Because Gran's favorite pie is apple and now she thinks you two have something in common."

"Oh my gosh, thank you for doing that. I would have picked peach and she would have hated me."

Wyatt chuckled and tugged on one of the belt loops on her jeans. "Trust me. She's going to love you almost as much as I do someday."

Harper sighed. "I hope so."

He lifted her hat off her head and kissed her forehead before putting it back on. "She knows that I love you, so she's going to keep an open mind."

"I feel like the fact that we met in Vegas makes her hesitant to accept me. She really hates that we got married there. She thinks I'm one of those women."

Curious, Wyatt asked, "And what kind of woman is that?"

"The kind that gets married in Vegas to a man she just met."

"My gran reads people pretty well and that sounds exactly like you," he teased, earning him a swat on the arm. "Hey, she is not ever going to judge you for how we got together. She refused to be judged when she fell in love and ran off with her boyfriend's brother. She ended up pregnant but not married when Cal passed suddenly. She understands better than most that life doesn't always happen in a particular order. You know, like meet, fall in love, and then get married."

"That woman has lived a life," she said, clearly impressed with Gran's checkered past.

"Something tells me you will have a lot of stories to tell when you are Gran's age. Like the one about the time you went horseback riding for the first time. Come on, let's go."

Wyatt helped her mount Sunny before getting on Kingston. He had chosen the most easygoing mare for Harper's first ride. Sunny had been around a long time and was one of Wyatt's favorites. He'd had a talk with the horse earlier in the day just in case, asking her to be nice to his girl.

"Okay, I'm doing this. I am on a horse." She gripped the reins so tightly, her knuckles were white.

"Relax and remember, stay alert. I know you want to get on your phone and take pictures and such, but let's not forget you are on a living and breathing animal. It doesn't always do what you expect it to. You have to pay attention to her and to what's going on around you."

"No phone. Got it." The way she was holding on for dear life left little chance she could even reach for her phone at this point.

Wyatt made sure she had her feet in both stirrups and reminded her one more time to relax. "Keep the reins in one hand and slightly loose. You don't want to give Sunny mixed signals by accidentally pulling on the reins at the same time you're asking her to move."

Harper looked like she was going to throw up. "I am totally scared to death right now."

"You're doing great so far."

"We haven't moved," she pointed out.

"Give her a little squeeze with your lower legs and that will change."

Wyatt cued his horse to walk forward at the same time Harper gave Sunny the squeeze.

"Ah!" Harper's expression was one of fear mixed with absolute joy. "I'm doing it! I'm riding a horse."

"Good job, sweetheart. Now, stop squeezing her. Sunny's got the message that you want her to walk. Sit up tall, look right between her ears. Try not to look straight down."

Harper followed his directions like a pro. They headed for the western side of the ranch where he had put in the wildlife-safe fencing. Harper looked the part in her denim jeans and red-and-black-buffalo-check button-down. The hat and the boots were a little too new for her to look like she'd been to a rodeo or two, but she fit in just fine around here.

"Before you know it, you'll be roping calves and helping me drive cattle."

"Ha! Let's not get ahead of ourselves. I think slow walks like this are good for now."

"I will slow ride with you anytime you want," he said with a smile.

"Be careful, Cowboy Wyatt. You know there's nothing hotter than you sitting on a horse. I might start following you around all day long."

"You say that like I would mind. Honey, I'd spend all day, every day with you if I could." He meant it, too. Since the truth had come out and Brock was no longer a threat, all Wyatt wanted was to be with Harper.

He couldn't have accidentally married any-one better.

"Corliss would love it if I started working side by side with you every day."

Wyatt laughed. "Oh, she would feel some-thing. That's for sure. I just don't know if it would be love. I would love it, though. Being with you is my favorite part of the day."

"How do we stop these things? Because when you talk to me like that, I need to put my feet on the ground and my lips on your lips pronto."

"We're almost there. Show some self-control, would ya?"

In one short month, Wyatt had gone from a man who wandered from town to town with no plans to put down roots to a guy who wanted to tie himself to the woman he loved in every way he could. She once told him that she feared that if she stayed somewhere too long, she'd overstay her welcome. Harper couldn't have been more wrong. Wyatt didn't want to be anywhere she wasn't. The best part was she felt ex-actly the same.

When they got where they were going, Wyatt dismounted and helped her do the same. He didn't let her go when he set her feet on the ground. Instead he took off her hat so they could get to the kissing part she had promised earlier.

"Man, you're pretty hot on the ground, too," she said as they came apart.

Wyatt chuckled and shook his head. "You love me for my looks—is that it?"

"I can't even begin to count the reasons I love you. The list is endless."

He pulled her against him and kissed her again. It was time to do things right. The knot in his stomach tightened and his nerves were like live wires. "Well, I'm glad you said that."

He was about to rock her world. He stepped back and dropped to one knee.

Harper's eyes went wide and she had a hand on her heart. "Wyatt Blackwell, what are you doing?"

The surprise on her face was priceless. He reached in his back pocket and pulled out the small black velvet bag Serena had given him the other day. Inside was the ring that Harper's dad had given to her mom when he had proposed so many years ago.

"Your mom set me straight the other day

when I was over there and you got that call from your friend in LA. She said that if I wasn't going to sign the annulment papers then I needed to put a ring on that finger."

Harper's eyes were wet with tears. She covered her mouth with her other hand. "Is that—?" she couldn't finish the question.

"Serena said she's been holding on to this ring ever since your dad died, hoping that someday she could give it to the man who would love you as much as your daddy loved you and her. She said she believes I am that man."

Wyatt got a little choked up himself. Harper was full-on sobbing.

"Harper Hayes, I will never regret teaching you to play blackjack that day or marrying you that night. You are the best thing that has ever happened to me and I want to be your husband until the day I die. Will you marry me again so we both remember it happened?"

She laughed through the tears. "Yes. Yes. A million times yes."

Wyatt slipped the simple gold band on her trembling finger. It was a perfect fit. Just like Harper. He never wanted her to doubt that she belonged, she fit in, she was part of this community, of his family. He stood up and wrapped her up in his arms. They may have done this whole thing backward, but he didn't care. Wyatt's heart had never felt so full. This was the beginning of a beautiful life together.

Boy, would they have a story to tell their grandkids someday.

EPILOGUE

"So WHAT ARE you planning on doing about those two?" Elias wandered into the family room and plopped himself down on Denny's couch.

Denny was exhausted, too much so to chase him off. Another day, another twinge. Getting old was less fun than she'd hoped. She'd always had aches and pains because she worked hard and played hard. This was a different kind of ache. This one was deep in her bones. It zapped the energy to do something as simple as standing up.

"What am I planning on doing about which two?" she asked, knowing Wyatt had told him he was planning on asking Harper to get married again. Elias loved to have all the gossip.

"About your grandson and his wife. I saw Wyatt and Harper leaving the barn on horseback. That must mean he's making it official, huh?"

Denny had given him her blessing earlier in the week. There was no denying that boy what he wanted and he wanted Harper in his life permanently.

"Those two might be crazy for thinking they should stay married, but if I learned anything from my own experiences, it's that nobody should tell anyone else who to love. If Wyatt loves that girl, then so be it. I told him that after he gets done asking her, he needs to bring her in here and let me assure her that she is welcome in our family. I don't hold any of that stuff that happened against her anymore. She's a good kid. I can admit that now."

Elias scratched his chin with the back of his hand. "She was a wild card at first, but I think you got yourself an ace in the hole with that one."

Denny cringed at the gambling reference. She was no fan of that particular vice. The man she'd loved threw a lot of things away because of gambling. "She comes off genuine, which I appreciate. I don't doubt she cares about Wyatt."

"And they seem to want to stay in town. That's a plus for you. You're like me—you like your family close."

"It's nice that they're thinking about sticking around," she said with a shrug. She was completely downplaying how she felt about it. Denny was over the moon about Wyatt's decision to put down some roots here. Last winter, he wouldn't even come home for the holiday. It broke her heart. If Harper gave him a reason to stay, Denny could find a reason to like the woman.

Not that there was a good reason not to like her. She was smart, business-minded. She not only saw the best in those around her, but she brought the best out in others. Brock was a good example. Somehow, she got Brock Bedford to stop being a jerk. That alone was a reason to be nicer to her.

"Well, I'll have to offer up the Blackwell family guest ranch as a wedding venue. Maybe Harper's social media connections can drum up more business for my family."

Denny rolled her eyes and let out an exasperated sigh. "Always trying to figure out how to make something work for you personally, aren't you?"

Elias held his hands up. "Don't hate me because I don't pass up on an opportunity to enrich my business. You should look into this guest ranch thing. I wasn't so sure about it at first, but it's turned out to be quite profitable."

Denny had no intention of changing the way she ran her ranch. "You do you and let me do me. The Flying Spur is what it is. Once we are fully back in business, it will be just as profitable as your fancy guest ranch."

Elias leaned forward and rested his elbows on his knees. "That leads me to my next question. Can we talk about Xavier Howard for a minute?"

Denny should have seen that coming. Her older brother was here to meddle and there was no deterring him from that mission. She had finally decided it wasn't worth fighting him. Might as well use his determination to her advantage. "I plan on ignoring him when he comes back to me saying his final offer wasn't his final offer. I don't know what else we can do about him except spread the word that he's got all of Eagle Springs in his sights."

"The more people in town that you can

keep from selling to him, the better. I'll leave that up to you. The people in this town trust you. I think I should hit the road soon. Not for long—I saw the way your eyes lit up with joy when I said that," he said waggling his finger at her. "I need to go to Colorado and see what I can find out about this company of his. There has to be more to this story. Why would this man want to put your town underwater? Like I said before. This seems personal."

Denny cleared her throat. "I have never heard of this Xavier Howard person before this. I certainly didn't do anything to him that would make this personal."

Elias shook his head. "I don't know, Delaney, but I'm going to find out. My Blackwell senses are tingling and that means we need to stay vigilant. I don't think this guy is going to make things easy on us."

"Us, huh? Since when is this about us?"

"Just admit it. You like having me around. You like me helping you get to the bottom of this."

Denny loosely crossed her arms at her chest. "I never said that and I won't ever say it."

Her brother chuckled. "Oh, I don't need to hear you say it. I feel it. You can deny it all you want, but you don't hate the fact that I'm part of this family now."

He was so full of himself. Denny considered telling him that perhaps he should be wondering why his own family back in Montana wasn't begging for him to return. The answer to that was clear—they didn't miss him and she wouldn't miss him either. At least that was what she was going to tell herself.

"I survived sixty years without you. I can survive sixty more if I have to," she declared gruffly.

The man kept on smiling. "You keep sweet-talking me like that and I'll ask my wife to move out here and we'll stay forever."

Nobody was asking for that. Denny couldn't deny that she was interested in meeting the woman who married her brother… twice. The woman had to be some sort of glutton for punishment.

"All jokes aside, I do hope you come back with some answers because knowing the why behind all this might just help me sleep better at night."

Elias tipped his hat and she wanted to wipe that smug look off his face. "I'll take that."

Denny's eyelids felt heavy. She needed to rest. "Get on out of here. I have to have a nap before I welcome the newest Blackwell into the family. That girl talks a mile a minute when she's nervous and I make her awfully nervous."

Elias stood up and walked over to his sister. His fingers closed around hers. "Take your nap, Delaney. I'll start making some plans to get out to Colorado. You can count on me."

"Careful, Elias. I'm starting to believe you."

* * * * *

Don't miss Wyoming Rodeo Rescue,
the next installment of
The Blackwells of Eagle Springs,
coming next month from acclaimed author
Carol Ross and Harlequin Heartwarming!

Get 4 FREE REWARDS!

We'll send you 2 FREE Books plus 2 FREE Mystery Gifts.

FREE Value Over **$20**

Both the **Love Inspired®** and **Love Inspired® Suspense** series feature compelling novels filled with inspirational romance, faith, forgiveness, and hope.

COUNTRY LEGACY COLLECTION

19 FREE BOOKS IN ALL!

Cowboys, adventure and romance await you in this new collection! Enjoy superb reading all year long with books by bestselling authors like Diana Palmer, Sasha Summers and Marie Ferrarella!

HARLEQUIN
PLUS

Announcing a **BRAND-NEW** multimedia subscription service for romance fans like you!

Read, Watch and Play.

Experience the easiest way to get the romance content you crave.

Start your **FREE 7 DAY TRIAL** at www.harlequinplus.com/freetrial.